INCENDIO:
The Flames of Passion

SPANISH SEDUCTION – BOOK THREE

by Jean Maxwell

DEDICATION

For those who've traveled alongside me on my author
journey since the beginning, offered advice, reviews, praise
and encouragement, and embraced the El Mirador legend.
Salud!

Prologue

July 1972

The dented little pickup truck ambled and bounced its way down the dirt track that passed for a road. With each bump of the chassis, Tristan Flynn felt the body weight of his passenger lift and crash down again in the rusted bed of the truck box. He winced in sympathy at the pain this must cause her. But he chose to believe that the medication and injections must be making her close to numb anyway.

Jesus, he could smell her burned and infected flesh even from the driver's seat. Appalling, but he felt he could get used to it. Isn't that what they said about the American pioneers on the early wagon trains? To ease the noise of the wooden wheels grinding against their axles as they crossed the endless prairies, they used rodent entrails as a lubricant. Though atrocious, the smell was far easier to become accustomed to than the sound.

Juliana's body lay wrapped in sheets and towels, concealed under a tarp spread over the truck box. The shattered rear glass of the truck's cab made one less barrier between them.

Her presence weighed on his soul, as did the absence of Ariel Torres, Juliana's lover and Tristan's friend.

"Get out of here, now!" were Ari's last words to him two nights ago, before he ignited the carbon gases trapped beneath El Mirador. The hotel had gone up in a firebomb of destruction, leaving little time to save anything. Including Ari.

His friend had sacrificed everything; his life, his business and nearly the life of the innocent woman who now lay in critical condition in the back of his truck. Tristan held little hope for the unborn child she carried. Her reputation aside, no human being deserved to die by another's jealous rage. When Ari had discovered Juliana in bed with another man, right in the penthouse suite of his own hotel, he went insane.

The result lay scarred and bleeding not three feet away from him, and as he drove on, their destination rose from the dusty horizon. Zaragoza. What would her family say when her broken body was returned to them by an outsider; a blond gringo from Wales whom they didn't know from Adam?

It didn't matter. He would take her home nevertheless. He owed Ari this. The child might still be saved.

As he neared the city limits, Tristan noted the olive grove he'd been told to watch for. The road leading to the Sanchez villa lay just beyond it. He made the turn as carefully as he could, the steering column protesting with a gut-wrenching grind. Even so, he couldn't avoid the deep pothole directly ahead and his front wheels landed in it unceremoniously. He felt his cargo roll to one side of the box and come to rest against the wheel well.

He grimaced, and stopped the truck to check on her condition. The merciless sun beat down on him as he peeled one corner of the tarp away. A swath of her red-gold hair fell across the bandages covering her forehead. With a sharp intake of breath at the severity of her injuries, Tristan recalled that same red hair swinging in the air as she'd danced in the Madrid cantina the first night he'd seen her.

Ari had seen her too, and liked what he saw, because he had continued to ogle and grab at her throughout the night, leading to a bar fight in which Tristan had saved Ari from coming out on the losing end. Two months later, the fickle Juliana turned up at El Mirador, Ari's luxury resort on the Costa del Sol, looking for work.

The magnanimous Ariel Torres had given it to her, adding her as a central attraction to his floorshow. By this time, Tristan had hung around Ari long enough to know his generous side. A destitute student just graduated from the school of engineering at Cardiff University, Tristan had accepted Ari's offer to train him in the resort and casino business rather than continue his pointless backpacking trek across Europe.

He soaked a cloth with water from his canteen and dabbed her face gently. Poor reckless thing. She'd wanted to be a famous dancer. Now she'd be lucky to even walk again. If any good would come of this, it would be her deliverance of a healthy child.

Ari's child.

Despite her promiscuity, Tristan felt with unshakeable certainty that the baby was Torres' and no other. He settled Juliana on her back and placed the cloth on her forehead. It had to be Ari's. Only that would give the horrible turn of events any meaning. He closed the tarp and turned away.

Leaning on the side of the truck, he drank from the canteen. What lay ahead for him now? With his mentor dead, the hospitality business seemed distinctly unpalatable. He'd graduated with top marks in engineering, yet had no vision of what he might do with this skill. He hoped some divine intervention would make his path clear to him now.

He started up the truck and gunned the engine. The vehicle jerked itself out of the rain-filled pothole and shot forward.

*

"Basta!" Marlena yelled. Lupé stopped barking, but continued to wag his tail and jump excitedly with the other dogs. As a group, the canines all galloped down the lane toward the main road.

Marlena Sanchez brushed her dark hair aside and her gaze followed the animal's path. Their behaviour could only mean that a vehicle approached. But in midsummer there were typically few visitors, and Marlena could not hazard a guess as to who or what might be driving into her family's villa on a torrid Wednesday afternoon. She clipped the last cotton sheet to the clothesline and picked up the empty basket.

The dogs leapt and lunged at the beat-up truck as it inched its way up the drive. Marlena did not recognize the vehicle at all. She sensed trouble.

"Mama," she called toward the open windows of the house. "Someone's coming. I don't know who it is."

Bianca Sanchez Allesandro poked her head out of the window at Marlena's call, and squinted in the direction of the truck. The vehicle bore no resemblance to anyone's they knew. "Ernesto was supposed to bring the lumber today," she ventured. "Maybe he borrowed someone's truck."

Marlena wagged her chin back and forth. "I don't think so." The truck slowed to a stop about five meters from the house. She moved forward to shoo the dogs away and let whomever the driver might be get out and announce themselves. Lupé and the rest scattered at Marlena's behest, and she stood facing the truck with her hands clasped in front of her. The dented door creaked open.

A long, jean-clad leg stepped out from the cab, followed by a lion-ish shock of blond hair on the driver's head. This visitor was not from around here, Marlena concluded. He stretched and stood to his full height, nudging his aviator-style sunglasses up the bridge of his nose with one finger as he moved aside to close the truck door. He nodded at her.

"Senorita," he said. "Mi nombre est Tristan Flynn. Buenos dias. Esta casa de Sanchez?"

Marlena eyed the man up and down. He seemed young, though older than her own eighteen years. "Si. Que pasa?"

The blond stranger swiped his chin with the back of his hand. "Habla Engles?" he queried. Marlena nodded. "I've brought someone with me. I believe she is one of your family."

Marlena blinked. "Who is it?"

"Is there someone who can help carry her? She's in the back." He motioned to the rear of the truck with his thumb. Marlena drew in a sharp breath. Injured? Drunk? Who could he mean?

"Mama!" she called. In a flash, Bianca appeared in the doorway. "Get help, get José, or one of the other boys."

Bianca turned and shouted in the direction of the barns. Marlena moved toward the blond man. Though his eyes remained hidden, she noted the strong line of his chin and jaw, covered with a fine stubble that indicated he'd been away from any amenities for awhile. She'd never seen hair quite that color before, and so much of it. Its wavy curls stuck out in all directions, and she felt an inexplicable desire to run her fingers through it.

"Show me," she said.

Tristan walked to the rear of the truck, and began to unlace the tarp covering the box. "I'm sorry," he said. "But I got her here as quickly as I could." He lowered the tailgate and threw back the tarp. "Her name is Juliana. Is she one of your family?"

Marlena gaped at the crumpled form laying there, wrapped in layers of bloodied, sodden material. Running footsteps grew louder. José and Marco were nearing the truck at top speed. Marlena's eyes teared up at the sorry sight. How would her mother react? Juliana. Her beautiful and vivacious aunt Juliana lay before her in the back of a broken-down pickup truck. This is how it ended, the fearful nights worrying about her whereabouts, and the company she'd been keeping. Marlena's stomach heaved.

"José," Marlena said, as his running figure lurched to a stop beside the truck. "Get her inside."

Chapter One

March 1973

Tristan wiped the sweat from his brow and hung up his hardhat for the last time. The roadway from Zaragoza to Huesca lay complete after months of construction during the Spanish winter. His crew moved about loading the last of the barriers and temporary signage into transport trucks for return to the company yard.

With no money and no real plans after the El Mirador disaster, Tristan had taken a job with a local construction company in Zaragoza. At least it was one way, he thought, to begin using his education and add something, no matter how menial, to his virtually blank resume.

Road construction hadn't been his thing, though, and with an appreciation for those who had no choice but to do backbreaking labor, made a decision. He looked around the nearby landscape; while the traditional economies of the region remained strong, the tourist industry had even more potential. A relaxed atmosphere had settled over the country, with the aging Franco's declining grip on national affairs. Tristan could envision what was possible for the future, and he was going to build it.

Long, arduous months on the job left him lean and well-muscled. Lonely tedious nights left him frustrated just as the relentless heat made him thirsty. For more than just water. As much as he'd tried, he could not rid his brain of a particular pretty brunette.

He'd learned her name was Marlena. Her delicate frame yet determined countenance as she stood facing him in the driveway at her villa stuck in his memory. A juxtaposition of softness, strength, youth and maturity radiated from her. This seemed an unusual and fascinating combination of traits in such a young woman.

And it turned him on.

He supposed this fact was what kept him both in the Zaragoza area and at a measured distance away. If she was underage, the girl would be absolutely off-limits. At twenty-two, Tristan thought she might even consider him too old to even look at.

But time would change things. It had been eight months since they met. He guessed she might at least be eighteen by now. But he knew little about the social culture here, and how relationships were pursued within the traditional confines. He had a feeling they remained strict. Perhaps they still applied arranged marriages. Perhaps being a non-Catholic disqualified him. Perhaps just being an outsider was enough to bar him from even calling on her.

He finished packing his tools and hoisted himself into the open box of one of the trucks that were headed back to the company yard. Five other crewmembers rode along in the open vehicle with him. As the truck jerked uncomfortably down the highway, the vibrations made Tristan's cock grow hard in frustration, exacerbating his unholy desires toward the girl that haunted his dreams.

Marlena. He pictured her standing there in the road in her white cotton dress carrying that laundry basket. The breeze lifted her skirt a bit, and he wondered what would be revealed if the wind were just a little stronger. He imagined marching toward her, yanking the basket from her hands and tossing it into the ditch. His little fantasy alternated between ripping open the buttoned front of her dress to take her pert little nipples in his mouth, and backing her up against one of the trees that lined the driveway. This version continued with him slinging his arms under her knees, pushing her legs up and apart, the rough bark scraping her back as she begged him to thrust into her fresh little pussy.

"Oy, Flynn!" One of his co-workers yelled. "Ride's over, man. Get your ass off the truck and go home." Jostled back to reality, Tristan saw they'd arrived at the yard.

Home? He didn't have a home, just the temporary lodgings the company had arranged. But he did have a purpose, now. And if he didn't have a home, he would build one. Perhaps one big enough for a whole brood of little brunette beauties like their mother.

*

"Marlena!" Bianca called. "It's nearly time. Get fresh towels and take them to Juliana's room. If you need more, tear up some of the older bedsheets. Make sure the water pitcher is filled and bring some ice."

"Mama!" Marlena called back. "I know what needs doing. I've been doing it for weeks now, looking after Tía. You don't need to explain it every time." Marlena dressed quickly, making sure to tuck a well-worn magazine under her mattress before rushing to her mother's summons. It wouldn't do for mama, Consuelo or anybody else to discover it, as none of them would approve of its content.

She'd flipped through its pages countless times, but none drew her attention more than the center fold, it's glossy surface dulled and smudged from thousands of fingerprints laid upon it even before she'd found it in the trash bin outside the farmacia. If what she saw was what the modeling industry expected of its stars, Marlena must not be afraid to imitate it.

She dreamed of being a model someday; but that dream would have to wait, at least for today. Juliana's baby was expected any time now, and as much as she cared for her aunt, Marlena really didn't want to miss classes for the event. Final exams were only weeks away, her passage of which would secure her entrance eligibility into University. Though she'd dreamed of nothing else but a modeling career her whole life, a degree would at least provide her with a choice of other vocations to pursue. Perhaps Aunt Juliana might give birth in the next 30 minutes; then Marlena could be on her way to school as though nothing had happened.

Ernesto would be waiting for her at the bus stop as always. Ernesto Alvarez lived nearby and attended the same school as Marlena. In fact, they'd attended all the same schools together growing up. She couldn't recall a time when she hadn't known Ernesto. Tall and slim, he'd grown into what many of her class mates considered a very handsome boy. With his curly dark hair and penetrating brown eyes, she noted that he turned a lot of girls' heads.

But Marlena didn't see him that way. To her, he would always be just Ernesto, the boy who'd been her playmate and confidante for as long as she could remember.

Sweeping her long hair into a ponytail, Marlena hurried to her aunt Juliana's room to check on supplies as her mother had asked. Her poor tía. She lay on her side, holding her very pregnant belly with both hands. Her chest rose and fell as she breathed, working through another contraction. Was it as painful as it looked, Marlena wondered? If so, her tía never seemed to let on; but then, pain had been her constant companion since the awful accident. Perhaps she just didn't react to it anymore.

Juliana had spent nearly her entire pregnancy healing from the burns she'd sustained in some sort of hotel fire on the coast. Her scars were still red and raw, but she looked much better than the day she'd been brought home.

Marlena considered that day, and recalled the bushy blond-haired boy driving the truck that carried her aunt home. She'd never seen him before or since, yet found those fleeting minutes in his presence inexplicably memorable. His strange accent threw her off; she'd heard British people speak, as there were a fair number of them that vacationed in Spain now that the government had opened the gates to more travelers. But his voice sounded distinctly different, and the time had not been right to interrogate him further, given the urgency of his visit.

In fact, she wasn't certain she remembered his name, though he must have spoken it. Flint, or something. His Spanish certainly wasn't fluent. In any case, they owed him a debt of gratitude for bringing Juliana home, and he'd disappeared so quickly. She liked to think he'd turn up to check on his passenger one day, and they could all thank him accordingly.

Juliana let out a low groan, and Marlena moved quickly to the head of the bed. "Tía, is it time?" she asked. "Shall I get mama and the doula?"

Her aunt made a sharper noise and her scarred faced puckered into a wretched grimace. She nodded in a short, jerking motion. Marlena ran from the room.

"Mama! Tía said to send for the doula!" She rushed down the hall to find her mother Bianca, nearly crashing into her at the intersection of the hallway and kitchen.

Bianca grabbed her daughter by the shoulders. "I've already sent for her," Bianca said. "I'm afraid you'll have to stay home today." Marlena sighed and nodded. Bianca tipped her daughter's chin upward and looked into her eyes. "I need you here to help. We'll call the school later, si?" She smiled in that way that only mothers can, making their child both disappointed yet hopeful in the same instant. "Bien," she said, and dismissed her with a reassuring tap on the arm. "Go shoo the boys out of the house and tell them not to come back until we say."

Marlena ducked into the kitchen where José stood pulling cookies from a jar for his lunch. "José! Hands off the cookies. You have to leave now, my tía is having her baby."

José dropped the last cookie from his hand back into the jar and looked at Marlena wide-eyed. "Mierda!" he swore, but failed to move from his spot.

"Vamos!" Marlena shouted, waving him away with both hands. José turned and bolted out the back door. "Take the boys with you…and don't come back until we say." She followed him out into the courtyard and saw Marco, another of their workers, join him from one of the adjacent outbuildings. The pair of them headed toward the barn.

Marlena continued through the house, scattering any members of the hired help that weren't essential to the birthing process. José, Marco and about ten others worked for the family inside the villa, on either a full or part time basis. The traditional home of the Sanchez family, the colonial-style villa had stood on this land for a hundred years. Only by favor of the Nationalist government had they been able to retain it. Many country people had fled to other parts of Europe to make a living. While pervasive and ingrained in her daily life, tradition held little interest for Marlena. She'd just as soon leave this old-fashioned lifestyle behind for the big city at her first opportunity. I'm eighteen now, she reminded herself. I want to see and do things no one in this place has ever seen. She wanted to be a model, and models belonged in the modeling school in Madrid. Not the dusty farmyards of central Spain. She had already made her application to the school, but heard nothing. For today, though, she would be missing her regular high school classes to tend to her aunt and the coming baby.

Facing the main window of the home's entrance, Marlena saw Ángelina, the doula, approaching the house. A doula was another part of "tradition." Similar to a midwife, the doula was a birthing assistant, though not hands-on with the actual delivery. The doula coached and saw to it that the birthing mother's wishes were carried out, such as no drugs, who was allowed to be present, and the naming of the child.

Marlena snorted. Her aunt should be in a hospital, receiving professional medical care, not left to the back-room ministrations of folk healers. It was the seventies, not the seventeen hundreds, and Marlena considered herself a very modern young woman. Capable and deserving of a life of her own, unbound by the ubiquitous "tradition" that stifled society, and women particularly, under the Francoist regime she'd known all her life.

Besides, the hospitals may have been able to perform skin grafts, and preserve at least some of her aunt's youthful beauty. In this regard too, tradition reared its depressing head. Being pregnant and unmarried, Juliana had brought shame to the family and therefore had been kept hidden away here on the farm, and her scars accepted as a fitting punishment for her sins. And what of the child? How would he or she be treated by the family and society?

As Ángelina stepped onto the verandah, Marlena made a promise to herself. Her newborn cousin would not be shunned. She would make certain of it, take the child under her own wing if necessary. If she could become successful, earn a good living as a model, she would always provide comfort and support for this new little person that waited to be born, despite the odds against it, in the next room.

Chapter Two

"So, it's a boy, then?" Ernesto asked. He pushed back and forth with his foot, swaying the porch swing on which they sat side by side. Dusk shrouded the courtyard, and would soon dissolve into night.

Marlena nodded. "Si, a boy. A perfect little boy. She named him Jorge." Her eyes began to fill with tears.

"What?" Ernesto said. "Why does that make you sad? What could be happier than a healthy little baby?" He cocked his curly head to one side, his eyes searching hers from behind his wireframed eyeglasses.

Marlena's lips twitched in frustration. "It's because he's perfect, and the world isn't."

Ernesto laughed. "Well, that's nothing new. Come on, why are you being so emotional?"

Marlena turned to Ernesto, her friend, her playmate, her keeper of secrets. "I want to get out of here. We're going to graduate in less than a month. Let's move away together. I want to go to University or modeling school in Madrid, and I want to give Jorge a better life than he'll get here, staying hidden from the world in the shadow of his mother's sins. It's not fair. Will you help me?"

Ernesto looked taken aback at her outpouring of words. He blinked his bright brown eyes and swallowed hard. "That's a big step, Marly."

"I know that. But you have to take big steps to do big things. Don't you want something more, something better?

Ernesto paused, then shrugged. "I don't know. I hadn't thought about it like that. I thought I'd just see what comes… you know. Like we do every summer."

Marlena's lips pursed into a pout. "That's not good enough anymore." She looked off into the distance. "I don't want to pick fruit, or mind children, or stitch hems for rich old ladies. I don't want to be like a slave, like a peasant, like…" She stopped there, biting her lip.

"Like me?" Ernesto finished.

Marlena turned and looked directly at him. His expression turned dour, pensive. "I didn't say that."

"But you thought it."

"No. I asked you if you wanted to move away with me. Become something different," Marlena said. "You didn't answer."

Ernesto adjusted his glasses, and moved them higher up the bridge of his nose. "I…" he began, then stopped with a release of breath. "I want whatever you want, Marly. I always have. But moving away from here…I can't see us doing that."

Marlena's eyes narrowed. "Then what do you see?" she asked. "Carrying on, working menial jobs, growing old with nothing to show for it?"

Ernesto regarded her carefully. Their eyes locked for a long moment, then he moved deliberately closer to her on the swing seat. Their thighs brushed against each other's. His arm slid casually around her shoulders. "I want you, Marly."

As he leaned in for a kiss, Marlena seemed to snap out of a trance and pull away. "Hey…" she said, halting his advance. "What are you doing?"

Ernesto blinked in surprise. "I was trying to kiss you, if you didn't notice."

Marlena exhaled a fuming breath. "I noticed. Why? You've never tried to kiss me before. I thought..." she broke off.

Ernesto sat with his body awkwardly perched over hers. "What? That I only saw you as a friend? That I wouldn't notice how pretty you are?"

Marlena drew back and looked at him with her eyes wide. She shook her head side to side. "No. I guess I didn't. I didn't think you could see me that way...we...oh no." A realization seemed to sink into her soul. "Now we can't be friends anymore."

*

The familiar olive grove lay just ahead. Only this time Tristan approached it on foot. He didn't know what to expect when he reached the Sanchez villa; but knew he had to stop there. Bringing the woman home was only part of the story. He had to know if the child lived. He or she would be the only link to his late friend Ariel Torres.

Dressed in the best clothes he had, which were few to begin with, he trudged on toward the gates. Jeans and a rugby shirt would have to suffice as presentable. Spring blooms on the vines covering the gateposts exuded their airy scent as he passed through them. He walked past the trees lining the drive that had figured so prominently in his private fantasy and shivered involuntarily despite the warm day.

Get those thoughts out of your head, Flynn. Or you'll do something stupid. He could hear the pack of dogs starting to bark as he approached. Would the brunette angel appear and shoo them away as she did before? They came now, from around the side of the adobe structure, yipping and yelping, nearly stumbling over each other as they jockeyed for position in the group, running straight for him.

Tristan stopped walking, unsure of his next move should the dogs reach him before someone called them off. He stepped to the side, ducking into a breezeway that divided two sections of the house. Flattening against the plaster wall, he ran a hand through his unruly mane of blond hair, allowing the shaded air to cool his forehead. The dogs seemed to have become confused at his disappearance, their fading barks indicating the animals veering off in different directions. He remained a few moments longer in the shadows, taking a look around.

Shade grasses and wildflowers grew between the flagstone slabs under his feet. His eyes moved upward to an adjacent wing of the house, and noticed an arched window with its shutters wide open on the upper floor. He caught some movement inside; what? Could it be…yes! The very girl that fueled his nightly fantasies passed by the window. She wore only a white bra as she stopped directly in the center of the opening. She leaned over the sash, catching rays of sunlight on her face, her perfect, round breasts in full view.

Tristan blinked, but felt unable to turn his gaze, or move in any direction he was so entranced by what he saw. He knew he should look away…but too late. She spotted him first. A split second passed where they did nothing but stare at each other, then the girl made a noise and drew back, pulling the shutters closed.

Tristan snapped to and bolted around the corner, resuming his approach to the main entrance of the house. It wouldn't do for the girl to sound the alarm at his arrival, alert everyone to the presence of a peeping Tom before he had a chance to announce himself and his purpose here. He lunged up the verandah steps and rapped the iron doorknocker. He stepped back a pace, breathing hard.

In a few moments, a middle-aged woman opened the paneled wooden door. "Si?" she said, her harsh voice barely above a whisper.

"Hola, I am Tristan Flynn, a friend of Senorita Juliana. I've come to ask about her welfare after the accident. May I see her?"

The woman, dressed in black except for a white maid's apron, trained her steely eyes on him. Did she speak English? He didn't quite have the vocabulary to explain why he had come. "Wait here," she said in English, after appraising him from head to toe.

Tristan waited.

A few minutes passed before another woman appeared at the door. Younger than the maid, but mature, and well-dressed. He recalled seeing her the day he'd brought Juliana. She had shouted orders to the farmhands. La dama de la casa, he assumed. Attractive too, now that he saw her close up. Dark hair swept up in a large knot and bangs combed at an angle across her forehead, a la Audrey Hepburn. The resemblance struck him a moment later. An older version of the very girl he'd just glimpsed in the window. Marlena.

"May I help you?" she asked, a polite smile lifting the corners of her mouth.

"Buenos dias, senora. My name is Tristan. I brought Miss Juliana here last summer. Is she well?"

The woman's smile grew genuine. "Si. I remember you. How kind of you to call. Please come in." She stepped back from the doorway and gestured for him to enter. "My sister is recovering well. We are most grateful to you for her return."

"Gracias. I apologize for not visiting sooner. I was concerned for her, but work kept me away. I…" Tristan stopped talking, uncertain of what to say next. He felt like an intruder. "Is her…did she…?"

"Have her baby?" The woman finished for him. "Si. A boy." She reached a hand out to him. "I'm Bianca." Tristan shook her offered hand. "Would you like to see him?"

"Yes, please." Tristan answered. "And Miss Juliana. She was in my prayers," he added, thinking the comment might buy him some brownie points with what he assumed was a traditional Catholic family.

Bianca gazed warmly at him. "We are grateful. Thank you." She moved further aside to allow Tristan inside the foyer. He noted the polished stone of the flooring, and the finely plastered walls. Dark wood beams supported the vaulted ceiling overhead. Very Spanish, very grand. His engineer's brain began firing as he catalogued the structural features. "Please," Bianca continued, leading him forward to an interior courtyard. Here the ceiling opened to the outdoors, pouring muted daylight over the space. "Sit, have something to drink. Juliana does not wish to receive visitors, but I will bring the baby."

Bianca nodded off to the side, and Tristan followed her glance to see the same maid, or whatever she was called here, standing on the far side of the courtyard, waiting for instructions. He found her voyeuristic presence, pinched expression and piercing stare a tad spooky. At Bianca's signal, she moved off to fulfil her mistress' request.

Tristan sat down on a wooden bench. He liked this courtyard concept; potted plants strategically placed to fit with greenery that grew right out of the ground. Squares of wooden flooring alternated with squares of white sand, giving the space a calming, indoor/outdoor feel.

He gazed up at the sky. He twiddled his thumbs. He shuffled his feet, noting the scuffed and worn appearance of the hiking boots he wore. He wished he had more money. Then he let out a regretful chuckle. Money. Ariel had given him money, plenty of it, and shown him how to make even more money at the casino tables. But what good had it done? Ari was dead, the fool; and the money long gone.

A soft sound from behind shook him from his reverie. He turned toward it, and rose slowly from the bench. Marlena stood there, holding the baby in her arms. God, she looked beautiful. Her long hair cascaded over her shoulders. Beneath perfectly arched eyebrows, lush brown eyes that sparked with emotion locked with his. They telegraphed her indignation at his Peeping Tom act of earlier. How could he explain it was only accidental? In spite of this, he felt his body drawing nearer to her, without having to even move his feet.

"My aunt has named him Jorge," she said in only lightly-accented English. "She loves him very much."

Marlena held out the newborn for Tristan to see. He could already recognize the distinctive features of Ariel Torres in the tiny boy's face, and felt some measure of restitution. He hadn't been able to save El Mirador. But he did save Ari, as he swore he would. Because he had saved Ari's child.

Jorge.

His gaze returned to Marlena, unable to take his eyes off the brunette beauty as she stood there, cradling the babe and humming a tune for him. In that moment, Tristan knew his true reason for returning. Knew with crystalline certainty, that whatever his destiny might hold, she would be part of it.

Chapter Three

Dinner stretched on interminably. Marlena could barely keep herself still at the table, her meal long finished. She set her nervous energy to work at smoothing the corners of her napkin into the flattest fold possible. Her feet swished against the terracotta floor tiles beneath her. Why had her mother asked him to dinner? It was torture sitting here, knowing what he'd seen through the window. It wasn't right; wasn't proper. And why had he come back? It had been months since he'd dumped off Aunt Juliana, like a load of hay, into their care. He could have asked sooner, sent a letter or telegram, if he'd truly cared.

She glanced sidelong at his curly blond head, turned to attention on her mother, appearing to listen with rapture to her words. Charmer! What are you really after? Her face felt hot, and an odd sensation settling between her thighs. This took her by surprise. Her restless movements turned to outright squirming.

Marlena felt a tug on the tablecloth and a sudden movement to her left. Seated next to her, she saw her aunt's head bob downward then snap up again. Marlena grabbed her elbow to prevent her from slipping off her chair as she sometimes did when falling asleep at the dinner table.

The silverware rattled against each other as Marlena tilted her aunt's thin frame upright again. All eyes turned toward the two of them. Marlena placed her arm protectively around her aunt's slumping shoulders. Juliana snapped to attention at her touch and glanced around the circle of peering eyes. "Estas bien, Tía?" Marlena asked. "You want to go to your room now?" She purposely spoke to her aunt in Spanish; not so much for Juliana to understand her better, but so that the lion-haired intruder could not. "Vamonos," she whispered assertively, rising from her chair and pulling her aunt along with her.

"I can get there myself, "Juliana argued. "I'm not a lisiado, a cripple."

"Por supuesto no," Marlena answered. "Of course not, I just want to help you." She glanced round to the others at the table. "Please excuse us, goodnight everyone."

Tristan immediately pushed back from the table and stood. "Buenas noches, Senorita. Senora." Although he addressed both women, his blue eyes fixed upon Marlena alone. It gave her shivers, and to Marlena's mind, not in a good way. She ushered her aunt out of the room as quickly as Juliana's limping steps would allow.

Not proper. Not proper at all, his provocative stare. He'd seen enough already, Marlena thought, and hadn't the decency to avert his eyes in a moment of respect. Her mother would have him escorted from the property before the plates were cleared if she'd known what had happened between her daughter and this stranger.

When she'd helped brush her teeth and change into her nightgown, Marlena tucked her aunt into bed. Her last duty was to apply the moisturizing cream to Juliana's burn-scarred limbs and face. As always, Juliana insisted on a coat of her favorite coral-colored lipstick, even before sleep.

"Why do you wear lipstick to bed, Tía?" Marlena sighed. "I'm tired of washing your pillowcases every day."

Her aunt's fiery green eyes flashed a warning that Marlena well knew meant, "don't go there, child." Aloud, Juliana said, "My lips may be burned, but they speak with the color of truth. Day and night," She snapped the lipstick tube closed and handed it to Marlena.

"All right. Have it your way," Marlena replied, placing the tube on the nightstand. "But someday, I'll have someone washing my pillowcases."

Juliana chuckled, a rare occurrence. Her gaze softened toward her niece. "Be careful what you wish for," she warned in her throaty voice. "It always comes with consequences. I'm living proof. I wanted to be a dancer, and I became one. But the price of your passions can be high, very high. Are you prepared to pay it for what you want, querida?"

Marlena returned her aunt's crooked, wry smile. "I would pay anything. Brave anything. Even fire."

"Mmh," Juliana grunted. "Incendio. That's how you'll end up. Consumed by flame, just like me."

"What a thing to say," Marlena said, wary of her aunt's reply. Her mother had always said Juliana possessed a wildness, an awareness beyond that of average people, and often spoke of visions and foreknowledge. Was this one of those times? "What do you mean by that?" she asked.

"The man who brought me," Juliana said, letting her head fall back on the pillow, but keeping her burning gaze on Marlena as if in warning. "He also brings great change. He knows the price I paid, and will be the reason you pay yours."

Marlena hoped she'd say more, but knew the conversation was closed and that she may never know the full story of her aunt's ordeal, or the newcomer's involvement in it. She stroked Juliana's brow. "Goodnight, Tía."

*

Although she did not speak or acknowledge him in any way, Tristan felt gratified that the woman he'd rescued all those months ago was alive and among her family. He watched Marlena and her aunt exit the room, his attention firmly fixed on Marlena's tight little posterior. He felt more like an intruder than ever, troubled by these unwholesome urges toward her, in addition to his unplanned view of the girl in her brassiere earlier. He wondered if she would tell her mother on him later. Or perhaps she was even too embarrassed to speak of such things. He hoped the latter.

"Senor Flynn," Bianca said, interrupting his thoughts. "Would you care for more wine?" She gestured to the open decanter on a nearby serving table, guarded by the omnipresent maid and her stern countenance.

Surrounded by members of the extended Sanchez family, Tristan glanced around the many faces at the table, unsure what would be considered the most polite response. Accept or decline? "No, gracias, Senora Sanchez. As delicious as it is, I must say no. I need to keep my wits about me for the trip home."

Bianca smiled, and lowered her hands atop one another on the table. "That is most sensible," she said. "Will you have more to eat, then?"

Tristan returned her smile and placed his napkin over his plate. "No, ma'am. Thank you so much for allowing me to dine with you. I can't remember a more wonderful meal. I should be going now. I'm so glad Miss Juliana and her son are well and in the good hands of her family. Thank you again. Goodnight." He rose to leave, deciding that her offers of more wine and food might be her way of asking for his departure.

His hostess also stood, and the beady-eyed server wordlessly disappeared from the room at her movement. "As you wish, Senor Flynn. But it is late. I don't like to allow my guests to travel in the dark. We are outside of the city, and the roads can be quite treacherous at night."

Tristan agreed with her on that point. The route into the villa hadn't been easy to navigate; in the dark would be worse, and quite possibly swarming with wildlife as well. But what choice did he have?

"There may be serpentia," she added, her smile fading. "Please, we always have room for overnight guests. You must stay with us, por favor. For your safety, and our peace of mind."

Snakes. Tristan shivered inside. The others at the table appeared to concur. "Stay, sit and eat," said an older gentleman to his right, possibly an uncle or other close relative. "Have more wine. We make it right here in our villa." Two youngsters at the opposite end of the table clapped their hands and chanted for him to stay. It seemed the Sanchez family wouldn't have it any other way. He couldn't escape the feeling of being inducted into some privileged inner circle. Stay he would.

"I don't know what to say. Such kind hospitality. Thank you." He lowered his eyes in humble acquiescence.

"De nada," Bianca said. "Consuelo's gone to turn down a bed for you. Meanwhile, do have more wine." She reached for the decanter herself and filled his goblet with the rich, red liquid, before refilling her own. She raised it in a toast. "To our honored guest, who has reunited our family. Salud."

"Salud," Tristan echoed, keeping his eyes on Bianca as he emptied his glass. So the maid had a name. Consuelo. He'd make sure to steer clear of her if possible.

"What's going on?" All eyes turned to the new voice. Marlena stood in the archway leading to the dining room in which they sat, the question remaining on her face long after the words had left her lips. "What are you all drinking to?" She seemed curious, yet annoyed. Tristan swallowed the last of his wine with an uncomfortable gulp.

"Marly," Bianca said. "Thank you for taking care of Tía Juliana. Senor Flynn will be staying the night. We were toasting our thanks to him for bringing her back to us."

Marlena took a few slow steps into the room. "Si," she said. "For that we are grateful." She glanced between Tristan and her mother. "May I have a glass, too?"

Bianca's smile faltered, but nodded her permission. "Of course you may, dear, you're eighteen now." She filled the wine goblet at Marlena's place setting.

Marlena took it and downed its contents in one pass. She raised the empty glass in Tristan's direction. "Salud," she said, then turned on her heel to leave the room the way she'd come, leaving all eyes staring after her.

Chapter Four

The reflection off the mirrored disco ball overhead cast white, dancing bubbles spinning across the ballroom walls. Loud flamenco music filled the smoky air. It felt hard to breathe, but Marlena inhaled rapidly as she twirled down the runway. The skirt of her sequined, full-length gown spun like a pinwheel about her legs. She'd made it, made the catwalk as a top model and her smile couldn't have been wider.

She stopped at the end of the runway, striking a pose as the cameras flashed. Breathless, she turned and strode back down the length of the catwalk, her long brown tresses caressing her shoulders as they swung to her practiced sashay.

A man waited for her in the dressing room doorway. He had no name, and his features were indistinct. She knew only that he wanted her, and that it was he who'd made the dream possible.

"Cariña," he whispered, taking her into his arms as she landed exultantly against him. "Tu es brillante." Then he kissed her, as full and beautiful a kiss as she could imagine. Her world spun into a shimmering vortex that enveloped her, then faded to darkness.

Drawing a sharp breath, Marlena opened her eyes. No glittering ballroom did she behold; only the gray, predictable shapes of her bedroom furniture, dimly outlined by the moonlight filtering in from the window.

A dream. Nothing but a dream. She shifted beneath her bedsheets in frustration at being no closer to it than ever before. The room felt hot and her throat dry. She threw back the covers and got out of bed. The floor tiles cooled her feet as she crossed the room. The heavy oak door swung open at her touch and she slipped noiselessly through the hallway and down the stairs to the kitchen.

She had no need for lights; she knew the villa by heart. A large water cauldron stood in one corner of the kitchen. As she plunged the dipper into the cool liquid, the overhead light snapped to life. Blinking against the sudden brightness, she looked up to see their mysterious houseguest standing before her with his finger on the light switch.

"Lo siento," he said, his voice rough with sleep. "I…I came for some water." He gestured toward her as she stood by the cauldron. "I see you've beaten me to it."

Marlena eyed him up and down. His bushy blond hair framed his face and he looked much younger this way with unkempt curls dipping forward into his eyes. He wore jeans but no shirt. She guessed he had slept in the nude, only donning his pants when he came in search of water. Suddenly she became aware of her own attire. A plain cotton nightgown with ruffles at the neck and a hem that reached barely to her knees. She dropped the water dipper to cover herself with both arms.

Tristan blinked and lowered his eyes. "Lo siento," he said again. "I would still like some water. Do you mind?" He edged nearer to the water cauldron.

Marlena moved aside, but continued to stare at him. He lifted the dipper and offered it to her first. She retrieved two glasses from a nearby shelf and handed one to him. He took it, then motioned to fill her glass first. She held it out with one hand while keeping her other arm folded across her chest. When both glasses were filled, they drank. After a few sips, Marlena licked her lips and watched him empty his glass. Her curiosity rose to the surface, emboldened by the absence of prying eyes. "Why are you here?" she asked.

Tristan finished his drink and regarded her with an unreadable expression. "To inquire about your aunt and her baby. You've taken good care of them. Something I couldn't have done."

Unconvinced, Marlena felt her mouth twitch. "What happened to her? Tell me the truth. Why were you involved? Did you hurt her?" Tristan's eyes opened wider. He seemed surprised by her pointed questions. "Did you rape her? Is Jorge your son? Is that why you came here? To see if he lived and ease your conscience?" She hadn't meant to become angry, but the more she spoke, the more she realized she wanted to know. Know who he was; what he'd done. Uncover his true purpose here, if there was one.

"No," he said, his eyes hardening. "I helped her. I saved her. I never touched her."

"Then who did? She won't say; she is too ashamed. Tell me, or my mother will hear about you spying on me. You'll be sent away before daylight."

Tristan set his glass down. "He was a good man, an honorable man. But he's dead." Marlena winced at this but kept silent, prompting him to say more. "He loved her. I swear that he did." Tristan shook his head. For some reason he felt uncomfortable retelling the story. "He got her a job there as a dancer, at the hotel – El Mirador. It caught fire and was destroyed. Himself along with it. I couldn't save him, but I saved her; and the baby."

"Why?" she persisted. "Were you not in danger, too?"

"He was my friend." Tristan shrugged. "I have no other reason."

Marlena softened her gaze. His words resonated with honesty. He was not a brute. Not the one who hurt Juliana. Perhaps he might be just as he appeared, and somehow this made her glad.

"You don't like me, do you?" he said. His abrupt statement doused her warming thoughts toward him. She had begun to like him, and the idea that he thought otherwise made her uneasy. It wouldn't do to become enemies. He might be useful.

"I did not say that," she answered, lowering her arms to her sides. She hadn't considered whether he liked her or not. It would be better if he did, she realized. Perhaps her thin nightgown was advantageous. He looked at her with a new interest, his eyes traveling up and down her lightly concealed figure. She took a step closer. "Have you ever been to Madrid?" she ventured.

Tristan stood his ground. "Yes."

"Can you take me there?"

"What do you mean?"

"I want to leave here. Go to modeling school in the city. I'll never get there by staying here, living this kind of life. Can you take me?"

"I don't have a car. I hitched a ride most of the way here."

"You drove a truck before. What happened to it?"

"It wasn't mine. I borrowed it."

"You can drive. All we need is a vehicle."

Tristan stepped away, in the direction of the exit. "I think we shouldn't have this conversation. At least not until morning."

Marlena bit her lip. She might lose her nerve by morning. A strange insanity began to fill her brain, born of desperation and the heat of the moment. She raised a hand to slip off one shoulder of her nightgown, and cupped her breast with the other. "Do you like what you see?" she asked, her words a breathy whisper.

Tristan shook his head and backed farther away.

"No?" she asked.

"Yes; I like what I see. I've seen you in my dreams since the day we met. But this is not right. You don't need to do this. Please go back to bed. Goodnight."

She stood alone in the kitchen after he'd left. She felt sick. Sick at what had come over her to expose herself in this way. Sick that he'd rejected what she'd offered…she wasn't sure herself exactly what she was offering. Sick that she'd blown perhaps her only chance to escape her small life. Yet his words hung in the air like a tantalizing fragrance. Since the day we met. He'd been dreaming of her? Had he liked her all along? What did he think of her now, now that she'd debased herself in front of him? If only she hadn't been so impatient. Maybe he would have helped her without such brazen encouragement.

Her mind full of conflicting thoughts, Marlena shut off the light and hurried through the shadowed halls to her room. She sank miserably into bed and covered her face with the sheets, falling into a troubled sleep.

*

She awoke to the sound of Lupé's barking. Slipping from her bed, she crossed to the window to determine what had upset the dogs. She could see nothing from her vantage point, so she dressed quickly and ran downstairs. Someone knocked at the back door. Marlena opened it to find Ernesto standing there

"Hi Marly," he said, pressing a finger to the bridge of his glasses and pushing them into place as he always did. "Sorry it's so early, but I…"

Marlena cut his sentence short by flinging her arms around him. Suddenly, she had never been so glad to see him. The events of yesterday had made her yearn for the normal, the sane. Ernesto was her anchor.

"Hey," he said. "What's all this? I've just brought the rest of the timber order, like I said I would."

"I know. I know I can always count on you," she said, still hugging him tight. Ernesto relaxed his stance, raising his hands to rest on her back. He neither resisted nor reciprocated. Marly sensed he was still resentful of her rebuff from the other night. "I'm sorry for what I said the other day. We'll always be friends."

"I'm glad, Marly. You were just upset before."

She released him and stepped back. "Can you stay for breakfast? I'm sure Consuelo will have something ready soon, come inside."

"Okay, sure," he said. "How is the baby doing?"

"Fine. Everyone's fine," Marlena said, nodding her head in resignation. "Everything's the same. Like always." She stuck her lip out and turned back to the kitchen.

Ernesto followed. "You don't sound fine. Are you still thinking about Madrid?" They sat down at the oversized kitchen table, its thick wood top scarred with years of service and burnished over with dark wax.

"More than ever," she said, remembering with embarrassment how she'd practically begged Tristan to take her. Where was he now? She didn't want to face him again; perhaps he'd already left. She smoothed her hands over the table's worn surface then looked up at Ernesto. "If you won't go with me, could you at least give me a ride there?"

His face registered disappointment. "Where? To Madrid? Drop you there like a hitchhiker? You wouldn't be safe…I couldn't do that, no." He shook his head as if that settled the matter. "What about school? We have less than two months to go before graduation. Surely you don't want to quit now, that would be foolish."

Marlena felt her frustration growing. "Since when are you the judge of what's foolish or wise? Right or wrong? You're the fool, if you think I'm going to stay here forever. And a bigger fool if you stay here yourself. Didn't you say you wanted to learn things, build things?"

"I can learn things right here," he answered. "Build things, too. There's always carpentry work to do, repairs. What do you think I brought that timber for? I'm going to help build that pig barn your mother wanted."

"Pig barn," Marlena scoffed. "Is that the limit of your talent, your ambition? A pig barn?"

Ernesto's brown eyes darkened. He took a moment before speaking. "Maybe you were right, Marly. Maybe we can't be friends, after all." She felt sorry the moment her words left her lips. She'd hurt him without meaning to. She didn't want to fight with him; she wanted to escape with him. He stood up from the table. "Thanks for offering breakfast, but I think I should go."

"No, wait, please." She went to his side of the table. "I'm sorry. Yes, I'm upset. But I shouldn't take it out on you." She reached for his hands and took them in hers. "And we're more than friends."

He seemed wary, but squeezed her hands in response. "You know I want to be," he said, his voice subdued. She laid her head against his chest. A noise from the hallway startled them both. Marlena looked up to see a figure standing in the kitchen doorway.

"Oh," Tristan said, taking a step back in the direction he'd entered. "Excuse me. Sorry to interrupt."

Marlena's heart fell to her toes. Madre de Dios, she cursed silently. Now this newcomer must think her a flirt, a floozy! The day had barely started and it was already a disaster. She dropped her hands and pushed away from Ernesto.

"Who's that?" Ernesto asked, a tinge of insult in his voice.

"Nobody. Wait here," she said, and followed Tristan's retreat into the hallway. He stood there, looking uncomfortable and glancing around for another exit.

"I was just leaving," he said. "Thank you for your hospitality. I see I'm intruding."

Marlena opened her mouth to speak, but Bianca's cheery voice rung out instead. "Good morning, Senor Flynn." Her mother descended the stairs, flashing a bright smile toward him. She looked sidelong at Marlena. "Marly, dear, you're up early. You must have dressed in a hurry. Go put on something more appropriate."

Marlena knew that disapproving look, and closed her mouth like a clamshell. In her haste she'd thrown on a ratty shirt and jeans that had lain on the floor in her room. She knew better than to be careless with her attire when company was about. But something in her mother's attitude struck her odd. It occurred to Marlena that just a few hours ago she was certain that Bianca would throw Tristan out on his ear for impropriety; now she seemed to be welcoming him with open arms. Hmph! She turned and marched up the stairs without another word, leaving Ernesto behind without so much as an introduction. Marlena lingered at the top of the stairs, out of sight from the trio below, and listened.

"Ernesto," Bianca said. "How good of you to drop by. I'd like you to meet someone. This is Senor Tristan Flynn, from Wales. Senor Flynn, this is Ernesto Alvarez, a dear friend of Marly's."

"Buenos dias," Ernesto's voice grumbled.

"A pleasure," Tristan replied. "Um, thank you again for your hospitality, Senora Sanchez. I want to get an early start, so I should be going now. Adios."

"As you wish, Senor Flynn; it was our pleasure to have you stay with us. However, I wanted to ask you something. Are you currently employed?"

A pause. "I am between jobs at the moment. All the more reason to be on my way, to find my next job."

"Well then, I had a wonderful idea come to me overnight. Don Giorgio, the pastor at our church, is looking for someone to help with repairs. You said you studied to be an engineer, I believe?"

Marlena's breath caught. What? She's offering him, a stranger, a job? And right in front of Ernesto, too, who she knows darn well could do that kind of work! Her heart pulsed an insulted ache for Ernesto. Passed over by two women in less than five minutes. How could she let this happen to her best friend? Aunt Juliana had spoken the truth. This stranger brought change with him; and perhaps not all of it good.

Chapter Five

The room in which he slept barely measured six feet across, its length not even twice that. In fact, it hardly met the criteria to be called a room, as it only had three walls. The fourth was actually the outer wall of a church. It more resembled a shed or a lean-to, if one were to get technical. And engineers were seldom less than technical.

Tristan made the best of it though, and straightened the sheet and blanket that covered his cot. He poured water from a pitcher into a basin that sat on a wooden washstand at the opposite end of the narrow space, and washed his face in it. Such were the limits of his amenities at the Dama de Gracia Immaculata parish church, and he wasn't about to complain. Free lodging and paid work were, irony intended, 'blessings' to a displaced and penniless foreigner.

He could feel the temperature rising inside the shelter already, though it was barely past sunrise. The closeness and heat made him uneasy. It brought back too many memories of El Mirador and that terrifying night he'd lost Ari. Confined spaces would be a problem for him forever now, which didn't bode well for an engineering career. For that reason, he'd been up as early as possible every morning, making repairs to the little church. What began with some minor wall plastering had now extended to mending and refinishing the red-tile roof. Not the most desirable job to undertake in the hot April sun but far better to be out in the open air than indoors. He had no doubt the good pastor would continue to bring other deficiencies in the building to his attention.

This spring seemed especially dry, and therefore hotter than normal. He pushed aside the slatted wooden door and stepped out into the bright Spanish morning. It creaked open on its ancient hinges and then slapped shut behind him, the sound reminiscent of the many roadside outhouses Tristan had the misfortune to visit during his travels on the continent.

Pastor Giorgio greeted him at the rear entrance of the tiny church. "Buenos dias, mi hijo," he said with his usual jovial attitude. Don Giorgio's portly frame filled the doorway, his cassock providing minimal disguise to his protruding belly. Tristan liked the man; his stature and personality reminding him of Santa Claus. He never failed to make Tristan feel welcome and appreciated.

"Buenos dias, Padre," Tristan replied with a slight bow of his head. "I should be finished with the roof today. What else do you need me to start on?"

The pastor smiled and placed a hand on Tristan's shoulder. "You're a fast worker, son. I never expected the roof to be finished so quickly. Come, have something to eat before you continue. You can afford to take the time." He guided Tristan inside the building to the small common area at the back of the church that was used as a kitchen, for meetings and various other purposes that didn't have to do with daily worship. A long table stood in the center of it, laid out with dried fruit, pastries and a pitcher of milk. The pastor gestured for him to sit across from him.

Tristan did so, poured himself a glass of milk and tore into a honey-glazed roll. "Delicioso," he commented, savoring the sweet coating of the bread as it melted in his mouth. "Are these from the bakery down the street?"

Don Giorgio grinned. "Panaderia," he said. "Bakery. And calle means street. You have an interesting accent. Do you know much Spanish?"

Tristan swallowed his bread and gave the pastor a look of apology. "Lo siento, I don't. A few phrases, but not enough for a long conversation."

The pastor interlaced his fingers atop the wooden table. "Do you like it here? Enough to stay for awhile? I know I could keep you busy with repair work. And I know others that could use your help as well. You might consider learning the language."

Tristan nodded. He did indeed plan to stay awhile, but not wholly for the reasons the pastor had just outlined. "You're right, I should. And other things about Spanish life, culture. Can you teach me?"

Don Giorgio wagged his chubby face side-to-side in consideration. "Por supuesto, of course, but there are better teachers, and I have my flock to tend," he answered with a chuckle. "Perhaps one of our Sunday School teachers might do. I will ask this week." He nodded in affirmation of his own solution. "Si, that will do nicely. Now, if you've finished breakfast, I will show you what else needs fixing around here. As an engineer, I'm thinking you need a bit more of a challenge than carpentry."

The pair ventured outside and across an adjacent courtyard to a charming, old-fashioned well that stood in the center of the yard. It looked positively story-bookish, with its circular brick sides and tiny gable roof.

"This well has drawn people from all over the region as a place of reflection and prayer. It is regarded as a holy icon, where religious pilgrims paused for renewal on their journeys to spread the faith. It has stopped giving water, however; and the locals take this as a rather bad sign. I'm afraid we may be heading for a drought this year. I suspect it's either a natural depletion of the water table, or something is blocking it. Do you suppose you could repair it?"

Tristan leaned his hands on the bricks and looked it over. "Was the water used for drinking? Is it safe? Has it been tested? How was the water distributed before?"

Pastor Giorgio laughed aloud. "Now those are engineering questions, if ever I heard any. If the water flow is restored, I'm sure it would need testing in any case. Yes, the people believe that to drink it is to become spiritually renewed; however, to bathe in it would be considered especially significant and life-changing. But that's a lot of water to be hauling by hand."

Tristan gazed thoughtfully at the antique mechanism, then smiled at the good pastor. "Si. Por supuesto. Of course."

"Aieee, you are learning already," Don Giorgio said with an approving smirk.

*

Marlena watched from a distance as Ernesto took another swing with his hammer. He pounded into the wooden frame of the soon-to-be pig barn with such force, she wondered if in his mind each nail might have the face of someone on it. Tristan Flynn? Her mother? Maybe even her own, more likely. Bang—the hammer hit home. Bang—again. Bang! She walked toward him as he stood with his back to her, immersed in his project. As she drew nearer, she could see the nail heads countersunk into the wood from his angry blows. Suddenly she felt as though she didn't know the man at all, his manner so different, or rather indifferent, ever since that morning he'd met Tristan.

A good thing that Tristan had left shortly afterward thanks to her mother's intervention. It had saved her the agony of facing him again. She hadn't spoken much to Bianca since then either, so miffed was she at her discounting Ernesto's obvious suitability for the job over a newcomer. How could she repair their friendship, and more, convince him at last to leave this place and take her with him?

"Ernesto?" she asked tentatively, as he held a nail in place and prepared to drive it home. He raised his arm with the hammer in hand, ready to strike. "Ernesto!" she shouted, before he could swing again.

Startled, Ernesto halted his motion and snapped his head in her direction. He gazed at her for a short moment, then turned back to his work. "What?" he asked, re-gripping the tool in his hand, appearing unwilling to pause for her sake. "I'm busy."

Marlena cleared her throat. "I can see that. Can't you stop and talk to me for a minute?"

He drove the nail into place with a single hit, then slung the hammer into his toolbelt. "About what? What's there to talk about?" he said, looking over the structure.

"You. Me. Our future. Our friendship," she tossed out the options.

Finally, he deigned to look at her. "According to you, I have no future."

Marlena winced. "I never said that! I said there was no future here, on this farm. Why are you angry with me for wanting something better? Not just for myself, but for you, too."

"I like it here," Ernesto said simply. He removed his glasses and brushed them on his shirt front, clearing the sawdust from the lenses. "I like you. I like things the way they are, or were," he emphasized his last word. "Why does anything have to change?" His voice took on a painful note.

"Everything changes," Marlena replied. "You can't stop change. Even El Caudillo, our President, has changed, now that he's an old man. And that is paving the way for us to change our own lives, don't you see? It's our time, our chance. Don't waste it."

Ernesto replaced his eyeglasses and looked at her in earnest. "You know what I think is a waste? You and me wasting time arguing…when we could be together. For real. Not just friends."

There it was, in as plain language as it could be. She didn't want to encourage him exactly, knowing he had romantic intentions that she did not reciprocate. But perhaps dangling some hope could spur him into action. "We could be together in Madrid," she said, biting her lip.

He blinked, and stared at her like a startled rabbit. "Maybe we could," he answered after a moment. "But first I have to finish this barn." He thumbed behind him at the partially-built pen.

Marlena's heart jumped. Had she done it, changed his mind? "Lo se, I know. How long will it take you?"

He turned to view the project. "We still have school, you know. We can't go anywhere until after that."

She nodded, a bit disappointed. If she had her way, they'd be on the road already. But he was right; she couldn't afford to fail her exams and ruin her chances for University, in case her dreams of modeling never came to fruition. But she couldn't think that way. She had to have faith in her own determination.

"Marly!" Bianca called for her from the house, interrupting her complicated thoughts. Marlena and Ernesto both glanced in the direction of the voice. "Come here, I need you," her mother shouted.

Marly wrinkled her nose. "I can't wait to get out of here," she whispered sideways. Ernesto laughed, and she couldn't help but join in. She had her best friend back. "Ya voy, mama; I'm coming!" She turned and sprinted to the house.

Bianca stood in the kitchen with Consuelo, tucking items into a large basket. "What's all this?" Marlena asked, noting the generous amounts of breads, cured meats, cakes and fruit filling the basket.

"José is going into town this afternoon to take care of some business for me. I want you to ride along and deliver this basket to Pastor Giorgio."

"Oh, is the church having a food drive again?"

Bianca covered the basket with sheets of newspaper and tucked in the edges. "No. I wanted to thank him for taking Senor Flynn into his employ. I'm sure he can't pay him much, so at least I can see to it that they both eat well."

"Oh." She didn't expect that answer. Her mother seemed overly interested in Tristan's welfare, but perhaps she was reading too much into it. Running this errand also meant she may have to face the man again herself, and that thought made her nervous. Thinking about Tristan Flynn stirred up multiple feelings in her. Embarrassment, resentment, curiosity; some she couldn't even describe. She knew her stomach fluttered when his name came up in conversation. Perhaps she was reading too much into that, as well. "What time is José leaving?"

A vehicle engine rumbled to life in the yard outside. Bianca looked over her shoulder out the window. "Now, I think. Go get changed. I'll tell him to wait for you."

Marlena did as her mother asked, and changed into a dress suitable for wearing in church, along with a cardigan sweater to cover her shoulders, then went outside to meet José. He smiled at her through the open window of the farm truck and gunned the engine as though preparing for a race. Marlena laughed, and climbed in the passenger side. "Yeah right. As if this pile of rust could outrun anything faster than a mofeta!"

José laughed too. "Mofeta? A skunk? This well-oiled machine?" He put a hand over his heart. "I'm offended."

Marlena shook her head. She liked all the workers on her family's estate. She'd known most of them since childhood.

José was about her age, and got along well with him; he always joked around and made her laugh. He would be one of the only things she would miss when she left. "Vamonos," she chuckled, waving her hand forward.

The old vehicle ground into gear and lurched its way to the gate. Marlena held onto the basket handle to keep its contents steady. As they turned onto the main road that led to the city, the ride smoothed out, and a breeze caught the edges of the newspaper sheets. Marlena grabbed one before it flew out of the windowless truck cab, and printed ad on it caught her eye. She read it, and re-read it, to be certain she understood.

Models wanted immediately.

No experience necessary - free training provided.

To audition apply in person.

It gave an address in Madrid. This wasn't the school she'd applied to. It looked like a private agency. With free training? It seemed too good to be true. Her eyes fixated on the printed words, the tantalizing offer bouncing around in her mind. She might not have to wait until graduation! And it would save the cost of courses, too. She folded the paper and slid it into her handbag.

Chapter Six

Miraculously, a slow trickle emerged from the open end of the pipe. Tristan smiled and exhaled in relief. He wiped his forehead with the back of his hand and eased himself upright from his crouched position over the mechanism. He opened the valve wider, and the flow of clear, sparkling water grew to a steady stream.

"Gracias a Dios," Pastor Giorgio exclaimed as he stood nearby. "Bien hecho, well done!" A small crowd of onlookers gasped and spoke among themselves. The revered well again produced the treasured water, with a simple turn of a handle. The Pastor collected a quantity of water from the pipe into a blue ceramic vessel, then Tristan closed the valve.

Don Giorgio turned to the people watching, and lifted the blue jug with both hands. "Bienvenidos, todos el mundo. He aqui, nombramos esta el Pozo Misericordia," Tristan said, repeating the words Pastor Giorgio had written down for him, in Spanish and English, that he would say when the well was opened. "Welcome everyone. Behold, we name this the Well of Mercy."

After some investigation, Tristan discovered that the water table had lowered over a number of years leaving the drinkable water out of reach by manual means. With materials donated or purchased from local businesses, he'd constructed a simple siphon system. A small pump brought enough water up through a pipe to a higher elevation, initiating a downward flow to a tap at a lower elevation. Once the flow began, the draining action perpetuated as long as the outlet remained lower than the supply. The quality tests revealed no contaminants, just a slightly higher salinity with the added bonus of high magnesium content. The health benefits of this local mineral water were perhaps part of the benevolent mystique surrounding the little well.

While not exactly a miracle, the reaction from the residents made it seem like one. A number of children and their mothers approached the tap with pitchers and buckets, while the Pastor did the honors of opening and closing the valve for each recipient to collect their ration of 'holy' water.

With his mission accomplished, Tristan dusted off his hands and strode back toward the Gracia Immaculata. The sun would set in an hour or so, and he welcomed the coming respite from the day's heat. Tomorrow he would start on the next project Pastor Giorgio had lined up for him, whatever it might be. He heard the sound of running footsteps approaching from behind, then a tug on his sleeve. He stopped and turned around.

"Senor," a young boy of about ten years said breathlessly. "Me nombre es Ángel. Puedes ayudar a mi madre?" He spoke so rapidly, Tristan couldn't grasp any of his words beyond "My name is Ángel," and "mother."

He smiled at the kid, and spread his hands out. "Lo siento, mi Espanol es mal, Hable Inglés?"

"Ahh," the boy said, nodding and waving his hand excitedly. "Sure, I speak Inglés."

In that moment Tristan realized this as an opportunity to learn more Spanish, as he'd wanted. "Say your words again, more slowly," Tristan said. "So I can learn. What about your mother?"

Ángel nodded again. "You talk funny for an Englishman. "Puedes," he repeated, "Can you, ayudar, help, mi madre. She has trouble walking. She thinks the well water will make her legs strong again, but each day it gets harder for her. We can't afford a wheelchair. Can you build one?"

Tristan looked at Ángel. The boy's bright eyes and exuberant energy belied his thin frame and worn clothing. He was probably right about being unable to afford much; just staying alive and with clothes on his back might be a challenge for his family. "No sé, I don't know." he replied with a chuckle. "I'm from Wales, not England. I've never tried to build a wheelchair. Can't you get one from the hospital?"

Ángel shook his head. "No, no hospital. Por favor, come and meet her. She's right over there," he said, pointing at the line-up for the water spout.

Tristan turned and eyed the crowd. "Okay, vamonos," he answered. Ángel led him to a startlingly young-looking woman, leaning on a cane and shuffling forward with her water pail in hand. Blond hair peeked out from under a madras scarf pulled around her chin.

"Mami, esta el Milagro, Él te ayudará. He will help us." The woman looked at Tristan with round, blue eyes that betrayed hidden pain.

"Mi nombre es Tristan Flynn," he said, unsure of what Ángel had said about him.

"Gracias, el Milagro," she said, dipping her head in a polite bow.

"What did she call me?" he asked Ángel.

"El Milagro," Ángel answered matter-of-factly. "The Miracle."

*

Tristan made it back to the church before sundown. After scouring nearby businesses and garbage heaps he'd collected three bike tires, a metal chair frame and some wire. A wheelchair couldn't be that different from a bike, he concluded. Simpler in fact, since there were no pedals or brake mechanisms to construct.

He had to smile at Ángel's enthusiasm and his willingness to approach a stranger on behalf of his mother. While he assumed his name must be a variant of 'Ángelo' or similar Latin name, he liked thinking of the boy as an angel, a messenger. He'd certainly been that for his mother.

Pastor Giorgio had already returned to the Gracia Immaculata. As Tristan approached the back entrance, he could see the man seated at the breakfast table inside. He left his pile of repurposed parts outside the door and stepped across the threshold.

A surprise stood opposite the Pastor. Marlena held her hands gracefully clasped in front of her. She wore the white cotton dress in which he had first seen her. It made his cock jump with the memory of what he'd wanted to do with that skirt, but quickly controlled himself. He was inside a church, after all. "Hola, Senorita Sanchez." Damn, he wished he wasn't so dirty and sweaty in her presence. What was she doing here? Was she alone? Had she come here with the boy he'd caught her in an embrace with the day he'd left her family's villa?

"My mother insisted on sending food," she said, gesturing to an enormous basket on the table. Her expression seemed indifferent, almost cold; as though she felt put-upon to complete this little errand of mercy. Tristan was at a loss to understand this girl. He'd seen first-hand that she could be hot as fire, but now appeared chilled as ice. In any case, given the boyfriend, she might be completely uninterested in him aside from what she felt he could help her attain.

"Por favor, give her my thanks when you return," Tristan said.

Marlena nodded curtly, and curtsied to the Pastor. "Padre," she muttered softly, and turned to take her leave.

"Vaya con Dios, mi nina," Don Giorgio replied.

"Gracias," she said as she disappeared into the rectory and toward the front entrance. Tristan felt an inexplicable surge of panic at her exit. How could she come all this way simply to drop off a load of groceries and depart without a backward glance? Was she still angry at his refusal to continue their late-night discussion of a few weeks ago? He never exactly said no to her. There just hadn't been an opportunity to think the idea through.

"Wait," he called after her. "Excuse me, Padre," he said hastily to Don Giorgio, and hurried to follow her path through the church. She continued walking down the center aisle as though deaf. "Marlena, wait," he called again. She stopped, and he closed the distance between them with a few long strides. "Thank you also, for bringing the food."

Marlena turned, but stood her ground. "De nada, I am simply carrying out my mother's wishes. Whether you eat or not is none of my concern."

"If you're not concerned, why come all this way? Why not send one of your house staff instead?"

Marlena hesitated, then folded her arms in a gesture of aloofness. "I did. José is with me, but he's busy with other duties in town. Don't think I made a special trip just for you," she said.

Her words stung, and Tristan's heart sank at the same time his irritation rose. He realized that he'd actually hoped—no, believed—that she'd come to him on purpose. Perhaps he'd caused a rift in her relationship with…Ernesto…the boy's name came to him. A stray vision skipped through his brain of this lovely girl spread out on his makeshift cot in the shed attached to the building. Her brown eyes watery and welcoming, and the crisp white skirt hitched up above her waist; the temperature around them so hot that tiny beads of perspiration lay on her upper lip as her mouth opened in anticipation of a kiss; her exposed panties damp with excitement. He forced the thoughts away.

"Very well. I won't keep you from your business, then. I suppose I thought you wanted to see me."

"See you?" Marlena repeated, as if the words were foreign to her mouth. "You've seen enough of me in any case; and that shame lies with me. I would ask that you forget all about that night Senor Flynn, por favor."

"I'm afraid you ask me to forget something that is already burned into my brain forever. Don't feel ashamed. You asked for my help, and I wasn't able to give it to you. I'm sorry."

"You never answered me either way."

"I didn't say no."

"But you didn't say yes."

"I hadn't the means to help you at the time. Why do you want to leave?"

Marlena exhaled impatiently. "I told you. I want to go to school in Madrid. I want a career. More and more girls are doing it now that the government isn't so strict; The universities are filling with young women. I want to be one of them."

Tristan frowned in thought. "Maybe there's a way we can help each other. If I can get a vehicle, will you show me around? Teach me more Spanish? I want to learn about the culture here. Then I could take you wherever you want."

Marlena's right eyebrow raised ever so slightly. "Perhaps," she answered. "What is it you wish to learn?"

"Anything. Everything. I'll tell you about it on the way to Madrid." He winked.

Marlena dropped her arms to her sides, a smile forming on her face. "Buenas dias, Senor Flynn." She spun on her heel and reached for the metal latch on the great front doors.

"Tristan. You can call me Tristan. Is that a yes?" he asked.

She pulled on the latch and the big doors parted. "Tristan," she repeated.

He didn't want her to leave. He wanted to see her again. An idea sprung into his mind. "Can you bring me something from town?" he asked. "Here," he added, digging into his jean pocket. "I'd like some drawing paper and pencils. And a straightedge, if you can find one." He held out a few paper bills as she turned to look at him again.

"I'll look, she said, taking the money from him. "But I have to start home now, José is waiting for me. If I can find any of those items, I'll bring them another day, is that alright?"

Tristan smiled. "Esta bien, that's good. Gracias."

She nodded somewhat approvingly, and slipped out the doors. He watched her leave, her skirt swishing as she skipped down the steps to the street. Damn, he would find out what treasures lay hidden under that skirt if it was the last thing he'd ever do.

Chapter Seven

"I'm not sure, Marly," Ernesto said with a frown. "I don't have a reason to go into town right now." He dipped his paintbrush into the bucket and smoothed the whitewash onto the finished siding of the pig barn. Even Marlena had to admit he'd done a great job on the little building. Though only meant for animals, the structure was sturdy, roomy and almost graceful in its appearance. Ernesto had a knack for the aesthetic, and his coat of white paint certainly added to the finished product.

"Oh," she said absently, swishing a pattern in the dirt with one sneakered toe. "Does there have to be a reason? Why not just go for fun? See a movie?" She knew the idea of a date might spark his interest, even though she didn't see Ernesto that way. She didn't want to lose his friendship again, and if that meant leading him on just a teeny bit, she'd find a way to make things right again once her goal was accomplished.

She could see Ernesto grinning as he bent over the paint bucket and nudged his glasses further up the bridge of his nose with one knuckle while dipping the brush in. "Are you asking me on a date, Marlena Allesandro Sanchez?"

"Do I have to make a date to see a movie with my best friend?" she answered.

"What's playing?" he asked.

"Do you care?" He looked up at her through his paint-speckled lenses, and she threw him a coquettish smile. "Do you?" she repeated.

"Not really. As long as I get to see it with you."

"Saturday," she said, not as a question. "Now hurry up and paint. Haven't you finished that thing yet?" Ernesto made a move as if to chase her with the loaded brush in hand. She squealed in laughter and dashed away. Marlena skipped across the yard and up the verandah steps before turning to look at him. He did not follow, but went back to his work.

Saturday. The day that might change her life! She bought the things Tristan had asked for, and wanted to deliver them as soon as possible. She was dying to know if he'd found a car yet. Even if not, she could try to help him with his Spanish, and make him even more interested in traveling to Madrid. The museums and libraries there would show him everything he wanted to know about Spain. And she just might short-cut her way into the life she'd always wanted.

*

It didn't look like much. The driver's side had a big dent, and telltale rust showed along the edges of the wheel wells and bumper. Still, it was what he needed; a utility van. Parts wouldn't be too hard to find when needed, and the engine didn't seem in too bad of shape. The dent hadn't actually cracked the powder-blue exterior paint. The vehicle itself would do nicely to haul parts and supplies, and in a pinch, serve as a crash pad on wheels. While he wasn't crazy about the color, the price was right. A friend of the Pastor had agreed to trade the van for some work on his house and garden.

"Test-drive?" Tristan asked the man, gesturing with his hands as though turning a steering wheel.

"Si, si, drive," the man said, handing him the key.

With a bit of protest, the engine turned over and rattled to life. Tristan threw the gear into reverse and backed out of the yard, creating a swath through the tall grass that had grown up around the parked van. The man certainly hadn't driven the thing in a while.

The suspension seemed in good shape, as he negotiated the bumps and rocks in the dusty lane behind the yard. Clearly the van needed an oil change, lube and some cleaning up, but as he rounded a corner to turn onto the main street, he felt satisfied that the vehicle would suit his needs. No sooner had he entered the wider roadway of the main street, calle, he reminded himself, he found his route blocked by a giant tree. It stood directly ahead, planted conspicuously in the middle of a cobblestone square that connected with other streets. He stepped on the brake, but the vehicle didn't slow down. He pumped the brake pedal two more times then leaned his full weight on it before the van lurched to a halt, its grille just inches from the ancient, ribbed tree trunk that measured easily three feet across. Shit, a brake job would cost money, and what the hell was this tree doing in the middle of a bloody intersection?

Its black bark was rough and pitted, pieces of it peeled off and scattered on the ground below. A sagging rope fence laced around the tree, but his wheels had torn the cord in half. The tree's mammoth roots heaved up through the earth surrounding its base, the resulting humps more likely responsible for his stoppage than his brakes. He looked upward, taking in the sight of the entire tree, its leafless branches spreading out in a dark, wiry canopy overhead.

The tree looked dead. Perhaps the Pastor's prediction of a drought was correct. Startled passersby stopped in the middle of whatever daily business they had been going about to rubberneck at the scene. A few ventured forward in concern, children held back in their parent's grasp, while others drew nearer. Tristan got out of the van, knowing he would need to explain himself to the approaching onlookers.

"You okay, senor?" asked one man in farmer's coveralls. He looked at Tristan, but soon turned his eyes to the gigantic tree. He stepped over to it and touched the trunk, as though inspecting it for damage. Tristan worried more about the ruddy van, and crouched to examine the front of the vehicle and the tires. He hadn't struck the tree, thankfully, and the gnarled roots hadn't given him a flat tire.

"Buena suerte you did not hit the tree," the farmer man said.

"Si, muy suerte," Tristan replied, stringing together a few of his newly acquired Spanish words to say 'very lucky'. "The van," he said, pointing to the vehicle. "Bad brakes."

Farmer man nodded. "Mucha suerte. Tu Ingles?"

Tristan stood to his full height. "Si. Lo siento, but what is this tree doing right here?" A small gathering of people shuffled in a semi-ring around the area.

"It is El Guardián," the farmer man replied.

A familiar voice spoke up. "The Guardian of Zaragoza." Tristan turned toward the sound with a smile. Ángel stood in the circle of people, smiling back at Tristan. "It guards the city," he explained. "Been here for a thousand years!"

"Has it now?" Tristan said. "How do you know? Are you a thousand years old?" he teased. Ángel laughed, which in turn caused a titter among the crowd. He turned back to the farmer man. "I'll move the van, please stand back." As the people dispersed, Tristan motioned to Ángel. "Get in, if you want. Do you live close by?"

Ángel needed no urging. He happily trotted over to the vehicle and climbed in. "You be in big trouble if you hit that tree."

"Why? It looks dead to me," Tristan asked as he climbed in the driver's seat. "It should be dug up and removed."

Ángel looked at him in horror. "No, no, It is El Guardián… it can't die."

"Why doesn't it have leaves, then? It's a hazard, in the middle of the road like that."

"Everyone knows it will live forever! It guards the city, it's older than the city!"

"Who told you that?"

"My mother. She said El Guardián wasn't always in the middle of the road. It's the other way around – the road is in the middle of El Guardián! The city grew around it. It used to mark the entrance to town, before there were houses. Before there were even people!" Ángel exclaimed.

Tristan backed the van away from the tree, the two of them bouncing in their seats as it crawled slowly over the monstrous roots. The van's brakes were weak, but functional if he applied them hard enough. The boy made the tree sound like some prehistoric deity. "You mean like a thousand years ago?" Tristan said with a smirk. "I think people have been here longer than that. Can you count to one thousand?"

Ángel shrugged. "It's a lot, that's all I know."

"Well, the tree still doesn't have any leaves. Why is that?"

"I don't know. Some say it's a bad year." Ángel glanced sideways at Tristan, then out the window. "That something bad will happen. I hope it gets leaves soon." He pointed at a confectionery store as they passed it on the street. "Let me out here."

"Okay," Tristan said and pulled over.

"Senor Milagro, have you built the wheelchair you promised?" Ángel asked as he slid out of the passenger side.

Tristan smiled. His to-do list seemed to be getting longer and longer. "I'm nearly finished," he lied, making a mental note to give that project priority. "But call me Tristan. I'm no milagro, that's for sure."

"Okay, Tris…Tristran," the boy stumbled over the unusual name. "Think what you want, everyone else calls you El Milagro. Adios!"

Tristan thought about the tree as he drove around the block and back toward the home of the van's owner. With roots like that, surely the specimen could be revived, unless it was simply at the end of its lifespan. Impossible to say without knowing the variety. If drought conditions prevailed, the tree would have the same problem as the well, unable to reach the declining water table. It occurred to him that perhaps he could tap into the well mechanism and divert water to the tree through a pipe system the same way.

He found the van's owner standing in his weedy, grassed yard awaiting his return. "You like?" the man called to him as he pulled up.

"Needs brakes. You fix them?"

The man considered it, then nodded. "Si. I fix. Manana."

"Okay," Tristan said. "I'll bring it back tomorrow." With that, he drove off toward the Gracia Immaculata to show Pastor Giorgio their new acquisition.

Chapter Eight

True to his word, the man had fixed the brakes on his van the next day. Tristan drove it back to the Gracia Immaculata with pride. Once he'd finished running a few errands for Don Giorgio, he'd be free for the day, and could attend the Saturday market. He wanted to get some new clothes, locally handmade, to continue his immersion into Zaragozan community life.

As he pulled up to the church, an unfamiliar vehicle took up most of the available parking space. Annoyed, he maneuvered alongside the 1950s vintage truck and cut the engine. The van rattled and shook with some afterburn before coming to a halt. He clucked his tongue in frustration. It still needed some work. He entered the church from the back as usual, to find Don Giorgio, Marlena and—the boyfriend—seated at the table. What was his name again? Ernesto.

"Good morning, Tristan," Don Giorgio beamed. "We have visitors again, as you can see."

"Good morning," Tristan replied, nodding to Marlena and Ernesto. "What brings you both here?"

Marlena placed a shopping bag on the table. "The items you asked me to buy," she said, a coquettish grin on her face. "I hcpe I got everything right."

Her expression made him happy, and Tristan returned her smile. If she came here especially on his account, it made him happier still. He was excited to tell her about the new vehicle, and that they could soon go to Madrid as they'd planned. "Gracias," he replied, reaching for the bag to take a look inside. Everything was there; the pencils, the paper and the metal straightedge, just as ordered. He wondered what it had cost. "Did I give you enough money?" he asked Marlena. He certainly didn't want her spending her own money on him.

"Oh yes, more than enough. Your cambio," she replied, digging into her handbag for change.

"Keep it, please. There can't be much left over. A little something for your trouble, at least."

"Gracias," Marlena replied, the shy grin reappearing on her pretty face, framed by her glossy brown locks. Her hair looked particularly shiny today, one side pinned back with a barrette. She'd worn a different dress today too, made of a red floral print fabric. Suddenly, it struck him that she and Ernesto might be on a date, and her mysterious smile was for him, and not Tristan. Something seemed to fall inside him at the notion.

"We're going to the movies," Ernesto piped up.

"What's playing?" Tristan asked, more out of politeness than curiosity.

Ernesto glanced over at Marlena, a look of deep affection in his eyes. It couldn't be missed. He was definitely in love with the girl. But was she in love with him? Tristan wondered. "We don't know," Ernesto laughed, taking her hand. "We're just going."

So, they were on a date after all. Tristan folded his arms in resignation and walked to the other side of the room to grab an orange out of a bowl. His stomach growled. He hadn't eaten yet today. "Why don't you come along, Senor Flynn?" Marlena asked. "If the film has English subtitles, it might be a good way to learn more of our language."

"An excellent idea," Don Giorgio chortled, oblivious to Ernesto's thinly veiled scowl. "You should go, Tristan; enjoy the company of people your own age, instead of a boring el Viejo like myself."

"You're not old, Padre," Marlena objected. "You're wise."

Tristan concentrated on peeling his orange. "Gracias por su invitación," he offered, doing his best to use the language of the land whenever he could. Would it impress Marlena? "But I have plans to go to the market today." He had no intention of becoming a third wheel in their private excursion.

"The market, yes!" Marlena exclaimed, with a clap of her hands. "I'd forgotten. We should go to the market, Ernesto. Instead of the movie."

Ernesto's brows knitted together, turning his face directly toward Marlena. "But it was your idea to see a movie, Marly. We can go to the market any time." Clearly, he was not loving the idea of giving up some alone time with her, or a sudden change of plans.

"I know but, it would be impolite not to show a newcomer around town. I'm proud of our town, aren't you?" Marlena argued.

Ernesto heaved a sigh, and clasped Marlena's hand a little tighter. "Of course, I am. If it's what you'd prefer, we can go to the market. Whatever you want, Marly."

Well, she certainly had Ernesto wrapped around her little finger, Tristan observed. The man was moonstruck, for sure. Marlena seemed eager to include Tristan in their plans. It didn't make sense that she'd make a special trip to see a movie with Ernesto, then brush him off just like that. Unless… it wasn't her intention to go to the movies in the first place. Maybe she wanted something else. He almost began to feel sorry for Ernesto.

Almost.

"Don't change your plans on my account," Tristan said. "I like roaming around on my own time. Besides, I may need to get some more parts for my new van."

Marlena's brown eyes lit up, and Don Giorgio clapped his hands. "You got the brakes fixed?" he asked. "Muy bien, I could use a ride. I promised some of the rural parishioners a visit today."

"Sure, Padre. We can leave right away, if you like."

"You bought a van?" Marlena asked. "Where is it?"

"Come have a look," Tristan said, motioning outside with a tilt of his head.

Ernesto rose from his seat along with Marlena and followed Tristan outside. The three of them circled the rusty blue van, scrutinizing every ding and chip. "It's pretty old, but the previous owner is a mechanic and repaired all the major stuff. It'll be fine for what we need," Tristan explained. As Ernesto bent down to inspect the tires, Marlena stepped closer to Tristan.

"Is it reliable? For a long trip?" she asked, her voice low.

Tristan shrugged. "I guess we'll find out when we take one. But I think so."

Marlena nodded and stepped back a pace as Ernesto straightened and came toward them. "You may need new tires soon," he said, frowning. "Not much tread left."

"You're probably right. But they'll have to do for awhile," Tristan said. "Well, don't let Don Giorgio and I keep you from your movie. It looks like he's ready to leave." He pointed to the Pastor's portly figure approaching them from the church, his overcoat slung over one arm. "I'll head to the market when we get back. Maybe I'll see you there later."

"Maybe," Ernesto answered for both of them. He reached for Marlena's arm to guide her back to their truck. "If Marly wants to."

"Alright, adios," Tristan said with a casual wave, watching her be led away.

Over her shoulder, Marlena caught Tristan's gaze. Without needing to speak, her thoughts telegraphed one word to him. Madrid.

He nodded and smiled. She returned his smile and soon disappeared into the cab of the old truck. "I'm ready, mi hijo." Don Giorgio said, coming alongside him and interrupting Tristan's thoughts.

"Si, vamos," Tristan answered, opening the passenger door of the van and settling the overweight and aging clergyman in the passenger seat. His mind skipped ahead. He might have time next week to make a trip to Madrid. But there was still one potential obstacle. Ernesto. What exactly did his and Marlena's relationship consist of? Clearly, he was protective of her to the point of being jealous; that was obvious. He was certainly eager to please her. Tristan didn't get the sense that her feelings were reciprocal. What would happen if he got between them?

He started the engine and pulled away from Gracia Immaculata as the Pastor gave directions. Tristan had to remind himself that Marlena hadn't shown any interest in himself either, really. In fact, she'd been downright cold on most occasions, except when she seemed to want something from him. Perhaps this trip to Madrid was no different.

Tristan knew what he wanted; and it wasn't only to learn more about Spanish culture. His intentions weren't entirely that innocent. But what did she want? With growing clarity, he knew that Marlena Sanchez was the kind of girl to whom men would likely give whatever she asked for. And if he wasn't careful, Tristan might become one of them.

At each stop along their journey, Tristan waited for patiently for Don Giorgio to conduct his official but informal visits, sitting in the van, drumming his fingers on the steering wheel. When it got too hot, he climbed outside the vehicle to stand or sit in the shade it provided. He felt amazed at each home they stopped at—realizing how the people living in these rural areas really had very little. A few chickens, a goat or cow; some grew gardens, others did not. The houses ranged from small but well-kept adobe structures to hovels that were barely more than shacks. Tristan shook his head. The contrast between this and the fast-paced, vibrant decadence of the cities and tourist places like El Mirador was truly stark. Guilt rippled through him as he thought of his time spent in such cavalier style alongside his flamboyant mentor, ignorant of how the majority of the country lived.

Most of the occupants were women and children, Don Giorgio having explained that a good portion of the men had left to find work in other parts of Europe. Those who had returned brought with them new ideas and continental values, igniting the rumblings of social change among the common populace. Change was always inevitable, and had already begun. He could foresee a sweeping economic and social awakening of this land, a land that until now had been steeped in centuries of history and tradition. Somehow, he knew in his soul he was going to be part of it; that by his past actions he owed it to this country to participate in its transformation.

At last, they returned to Zaragoza and the Gracia Immaculata, where Don Giorgio took his leave of Tristan. "Bless you, mi hijo; you have served God and my flock well today by your patience and kindness. Now, go and enjoy yourself in town."

"Gracias, Padre. I won't be long." The rotund cleric waved his goodbye and waddled into his sanctuary, leaving Tristan to his own devices. They had been a few hours on the road, but perhaps the market was still open. He decided to stretch his legs after the long drive and walk the few blocks there. Lively music and mouth-watering smells drifted toward him as he got nearer, and soon found himself in the middle of the action, the little plaza surrounding the stark presence of El Guardián alive with movement and sound.

Some stalls had closed up, but many others were still in business. He found one selling bright colored satin shirts, bittersweetly reminding him of the flashy attire that Ariel often wore. He moved along to another stall hawking woven serapes, ponchos and leather goods. He wondered if he could pull off the look he'd seen in the recent "spaghetti western" films. The girls in Britain went wild for actor Clint Eastwood, and Tristan wouldn't mind that kind of attention. At the proprietor's hearty insistence, he tried on a poncho and then of course felt obligated to buy it; but since his intention was to live like a local, it seemed a justifiable purchase.

He continued along the ring of stalls sporting his new poncho, picking out some decent jeans and a thick, hand-tooled leather belt. Working outdoors as he often did, a hat was a necessity and found a booth selling various western-style hats. He tried on several before discovering one that looked exactly like Clint Eastwood's. As he put it on his head, the savvy vendor smiled in approval, clearly assuring himself of a sale.

"It doesn't suit you," came a voice from behind. Tristan turned toward it, a smile brewing on his face despite the uncomplimentary words. He was rewarded with a view of the lovely Marlena standing a few feet away, arms crossed and looking him up and down in critique. She leaned to one side, displaying a tantalizing length of shapely leg.

"No?" he asked, tipping the brim down over his eyes. "How about now?"

She pursed her lips and shook her head. "You are no Clint Eastwood."

Tristan's eyebrows rose in surprise that she mentioned the actor. "Says who?"

"The film I just saw. High Plains Drifter."

Tristan chuckled at the coincidence. "Well then, I guess I shouldn't try." He returned the hat to the vendor's pile.

Marlena moved closer and plucked a different hat from the pile. "Try this one." She handed him a woven, tri-cornered number, which Tristan easily recognized. He also recognized the comely girl was teasing him. Was this her way of flirting, or did she hold as much disdain for him as her words intimated?

"Isn't that what bullfighters wear?"

"Matadores," she answered. "Yes. It is called a Montera."

Tristan eyeballed the black cap with its rounded knobs of fabric on either side of the ears. "I don't think my head's quite that big," he answered, declining to take it from her. She tossed it back on the pile.

"Have you ever seen a corrida, Senor?" Seemingly out of nowhere, Ernesto appeared by Marlena's side, a disapproving look on his tanned face. His tone suggested a challenge; a dare.

"A what?"

"A corrida—a bullfight."

"No, I haven't had the misfortune so far," Tristan said.

"Perhaps men from your country are not strong of heart. The sight of blood bothers you?" Ernesto continued, clearly trying to get a rise out of him. He wouldn't succeed.

"No. I just think it is a cruel, barbaric ritual."

"It's part of our culture," Marlena interrupted. "You wished to learn Spanish culture, did you not? Are you not a man of your word?"

Tristan felt his hackles rise, and also his jealousy as Ernesto intertwined his hand with Marlena's. "I assure you that I am," he replied, his voice firm. "There is a…corrida…tomorrow, isn't there?"

"There is one every Sunday," Ernesto nodded.

"Bien. Let's go, then," Tristan said, his gaze locking with Marlena's. "All of us."

Chapter Nine

Marlena wondered if the Zaragoza bullring would impress Tristan. If he was an engineer, as he said, he must have seen many kinds of structures and would no doubt be judging its construction as much as its purpose, considering his opinion of bullfighting. To her, the bullfights were simply another part of the omnipresent 'traditions' she had been surrounded by her whole life, and was slowly growing to despise.

But her feelings on the matter were unlikely to change the spectacle they were about to see. As they took their seats in the circular amphitheater, Tristan sweated visibly, the unrelenting sun bearing down on them. As the day wore on, the angle of sunlight would change and give them some relief, but the permanently shaded seats were reserved only for the highest-paying spectators.

The heat did not bother Marlena so much, knowing from experience to wear a wide-brimmed sunhat to these events. Her mother had always ensured she had one that matched her dress, ever since she was a little girl, and out of habit, did the same today. She clutched the brim as a rare breeze lifted beneath it, and stole glances at the men seated on either side of her.

Tristan, looking uncomfortable as perspiration beaded on his forehead; and Ernesto, gazing off into the distance with a defiant tilt of his chin. Both looked equally reluctant to be here. She knew Ernesto was trying to prove something; expose the foreign-ness, and therefore weakness, of their guest, hoping to demoralize him in Marlena's eyes. She did not relish nor appreciate Ernesto's behavior of late, which had all the signs of jealousy. But she had only herself to blame; it was she who forced contact between the two men, whether planned or unplanned.

Tristan too, had something to prove. That he was not faint of heart, as Ernesto had jeered; but Marlena could not shake the impression he thought very highly of himself—even superior to those around him, especially her childhood friend. Without meaning to, she had created enemies; or at least competitors. But competitors for what? Her attention, perhaps; but she sensed it went deeper than that. A ripple of guilt washed over her at being responsible for this uneasy situation, but trickled away as the sound of trumpet heralds signalled the start of the event.

The bullfighting teams paraded the arena to music, their incredible 'suits of light' on display. The brilliant colors and golden sequins flashed in the sunlight, and an electric excitement built in the air. Ernesto's arm curled surreptitiously about Marlena's shoulder, and she nudged it away. They were not on a 'date'. In fact, Ernesto's displays of affection had begun to irritate her. He'd especially begun doing this since Tristan's arrival. Was that the only time men showed their intentions? When there was competition involved? Did it have anything to do with their real feelings?

With this thought, Marlena struggled to analyze her own feelings. Did she dislike Ernesto's attention because she only saw him as a friend—or that she wanted Tristan's attention more? The truth struck a troublesome chord in her heart. She liked this blond stranger, despite her suspicions and hostility toward him. He was different. He was handsome. And he had the potential to change her life, in a way no one else could. Her pulse quickened. Her Tía was right!

She glanced over at Tristan, his mouth stiffened into a stern line, his muscular arms crossed against his body in a tight, defensive stance as he watched the action below. Did he still dream of her at night, as he said he did? The possibilities he represented were intoxicating. He did not need to stay here, shackled by tradition, as she felt. He dictated his own future, made his own decisions, which was exactly what Marlena wanted, too. It dawned on her that they were more alike than different, and it was a mistake for her to have goaded him and pretended to be so aloof. You catch more flies with honey than with vinegar, the old axiom said. Perhaps it was time to spread the honey, if she was ever to gain what she truly wanted.

*

Tristan's discomfort increased with every passing second, seated in the grandstand amid the press of thousands, the oppressive heat only one of many contributing factors. It made him think of the horrible night he'd last spoken with Ariel; facing each other in the darkened bowels of El Mirador, sweat and terror dripping from his skin in equal measure. He shook off the memory by sheer will, and shifted his thoughts back to the present.

Marlena sat next to him, looking blissfully unbothered by the morbid heat and more beautiful than ever in her pretty blue sundress and matching hat; and on her other side…sat his opponent. Tristan still didn't exactly get their relationship. He only knew he was determined to sever it somehow. With self-satisfied amusement he noted Ernesto's attempt to embrace Marlena's shoulders and her subtle brush-off of the same.

Hiding a smirk, Tristan looked away, focusing on the ominous tableau of color, man and beast in the ring below.

The fervor of the crowd, knowing what they were about to witness, stirred unexpected feelings within him. He did not understand blood sport; but a wicked fascination built in his mind, and a strange taste formed at the base of his tongue at the prospect of seeing it firsthand. He supposed it was some vestige of humanity's primal, savage nature that would never be completely submerged no matter how many centuries passed.

"This is the paseíllo, the parade," Marlena said, leaning slightly toward him. Her lovely floral perfume wafted beneath his nostrils. He'd never been this close to her before, nor even touched her; and now their bodies pressed against each other, creating a different kind of heat. One that built in his loins, and felt hotter than the air around them.

"It's quite a spectacle. When does the killing begin?" Tristan asked, mild disdain in his voice.

Marlena shot him a look, her lovely eyes narrowing. "It is not a simple 'killing'. There is much ritual and skill," she replied. Those men are the cuadrillas, the bullfighting teams. They are highly trained. After they circle the ring, we will see the bulls presented."

"Bulls? There's more than one?"

"Yes. A corrida usually has several bulls in one day, and a different cuadrilla for each."

Tristan wiped his brow with the back of his hand. My God, how can anyone stand to watch this? He hoped they did not have to stay for the entire thing. "A whole team against one animal hardly seems fair."

"If it is too much for you, you are welcome to leave," Ernesto interjected.

"Who said anything about leaving," Tristan shot back, refusing to rise to the bait. He kept his eyes on the ring. One by one, three gigantic fighting bulls entered the arena. The animals were massive, larger than any bovine he'd ever seen in his home country. Obviously bred and raised for a singular purpose, their huge neck and shoulder muscles flexed and rippled as they moved about the ring, sunlight reflecting on the ridges of their smooth, dark coats. They were nothing short of magnificent, and it seemed incomprehensible that by sundown, all would be methodically slaughtered amid thunderous applause.

Rich aromas filled the amphitheater, a feral mix of animals and humans, but also of flowers and fried food from the vendors below; a heavy, bloodthirsty melange that settled over the scene like a shroud. A death shroud. But Tristan wasn't going to turn away. If he were to have any stake in this country, or understand the girl seated next to him, he must observe, and learn.

Marlena explained to him with cool, almost bored detachment each part, or tercio, of the fight as it played out before them. Three men of the cuadrilla, called Banderilleros, thrust their colored capes at the animal, inciting him to charge so that the Matador could judge its ferocity, its strengths or weaknesses. Tristan chose to imagine the cheers of the crowd as praise for its grace and strength rather than the antics of its tormenters.

Then came the Picadores, mounted on horseback and armed with ominous, spear-like poles. The horses wore suits of padded armor, but the riders did not.

"This is Tercio de Vara, the part of lances," Marlena said.

"They're going to stab it?" Tristan asked. "I thought that was the Matador's job."

"It is the Matador who kills the bull," she said. "The Picadores simply weaken it."

Tristan's inner anger and apprehension rose. It was one thing to pit man against beast, but there was no fair play here—the outcome was predetermined and assured by multiple levels of assault on an animal who had no chance to escape. Or did it? "Does a bull ever survive the fight?" he asked.

"I don't know. I've never seen that happen in my lifetime," Marlena stated, but it was Ernesto who answered.

"It can happen. Occasionally a bull may survive the faena, the fight. The presidente may also free the bull if he feels it has given an exceptional performance. But it brings dishonor to the Matador either way."

"So, the odds aren't good in other words."

"No, senor. They are not." Ernesto replied, with a piercing glance through his wire-rimmed eyeglasses, telegraphing his insinuation that neither were Tristan's. Tristan matched his stare for a long minute, then turned away. A silent gauntlet had been thrown. More than Matadors were fighting today. He and Ernesto were in the ring, too, waging an age-old combat for the affections of a woman. Only one could win; and Tristan was bound and determined to be the man who did.

He watched in stony silence as the Picadores drew blood from the animal with blows of their deadly lances. As the bull charged at the armoured horses, lowering its massive head in an attempt to gore and lift them, the riders plunged their long blades into its majestic neck and shoulders. Soon, the bull became visibly damaged, its spilled blood seeping into the sand that covered the floor of the ring and disappearing as if it had never been there. Somewhat mercifully, a trumpet herald signalled the end of this phase of the fight, but also the beginning of the next.

The bull pawed and trotted its way around the ring, appearing disoriented and in distress. The crowd cheered and shouted their praise of the Picadores performance, unconcerned with the animal's alarming condition. But the ordeal was far from over. Marlena explained the next part they would see was the Tercio de Banderillas, where the Matador enters for the first time and attempts to lodge several colorful barbed sticks called banderillas into the bull's mighty shoulders.

With much flashing of colored capes and fanciful maneuvers, the bull was further induced to charge directly at the Matador himself, who would then thrust a banderilla into its flesh as it passed beneath the fluttering cape. Wild, enthusiastic applause followed each pass, and Tristan swallowed his distaste at the sight of the heavy sticks dangling from the animal's back as it spun and readied for another angry charge. The energy of the crowd became difficult to ignore, and worse, easy to be caught up in. His own pulse began to accelerate, the smell of the dying animal's blood carried to him on the suffocating waves of heat. The bull staggered as it tried valiantly to lift its great head for another attack. The scene was gory, surreal; yet he would not tear his eyes away. Soon, he too clamored for the animal's demise, and to his disgust, realized it was not only to end its suffering, but in anticipation of witnessing the final death blow.

The Matador left the arena to insane cheers, only to reappear with a different red cape and a heavy sword. Surely this must be the instrument of death, and the moment near. Noise from the crowd reached a fever pitch as the exhausted bull rallied its last ounces of strength to charge at his opponent several more times, the Matador trailing the red cape across its head and horns with deft and dangerous movements. Then, with animal and man just inches apart, the Matador plunged his sword between its shoulder blades, piercing through the spinal cord and aorta.

The crowd rose to its feet all around him. Tristan stood as well, but his parched throat had no shouts of glory to offer. "I need something to drink," he said, then stepped into the aisle and strode away from the seating area.

*

"Where is he going," Ernesto muttered as he applauded the marvelous estocada, the killing stroke, that the Matador had just executed. It was the best outcome possible, the bull receiving a quick and clean death by a skilful estocada. The animal dropped instantly, the horrendous pool of spilt blood quickly absorbing into the sand beneath its felled carcass. "Told you he couldn't take it."

Marlena threw an annoyed glance at her childhood friend. She'd never seen him behave so badly, or speak so impolitely of another person. She felt certain that Tristan had simply gone to the snack bar, hoping to get ahead of the rush of patrons that would soon follow. "He's thirsty," Marlena snapped. "And so am I." Without waiting for Ernesto, she rose and followed the path Tristan had taken, down the aisle and the stairs that led to the public level and vendor stalls. Dodging the milling people, she found him leaning against a wall that offered some measure of shade, sipping from the familiar pint mug in which beer was served. He looked up as she approached.

"Sorry, I…should have asked…if you wanted a drink, too."

"No, I'm fine, thank you," she said, removing her sun hat and tossing a length of her long hair back over her shoulder. She couldn't quite read his expression, or rather, lack of it. His blue-eyed gaze gave nothing away, and that piqued her interest even further. She wanted to know what lay behind the handsome face. And she couldn't deny it any longer. She found that face very handsome, indeed. "So, what do you think of the corrida?" she asked.

"It's certainly an experience," he said.

"So, you enjoyed it?"

Tristan took a long swallow of beer from his mug before answering. "Not exactly. But it was my idea to come."

"True," Marlena said, slowly fanning herself with her hat. "And did you get what you came for?"

His eyes roved over her, eliciting an unexpected flutter in her belly. She liked it; and liked the way he looked at her, as a street cat looks into a fish shop window. Desirous and calculating, working out his next move. "What do you mean by that?" he asked.

"As you said, it was your idea." She took a step closer to him.

Tristan set his empty mug on a nearby ledge. "It wasn't the best idea. But I think I did get what I came for."

"And what's that?"

He pushed away from the wall and straightened to his full height, moving within inches of her. "To get you alone."

The flutter in her belly began again. His nearness excited her, in a way it didn't before. Or was it just all the sights and sounds and spectacle of the bullring making it happen? "We're hardly alone," she replied, gesturing to the pressing throng of people all around them.

"I meant, without your boyfriend."

Her boyfriend? Is that what he thought? Ernesto was her boyfriend? With alarm, Marlena realized how it must look; not just to Tristan but many others as well. They weren't children any longer. To be seen with Ernesto so often would make people talk and get the wrong idea. The last thing in the world she wanted was to hurt Ernesto. But it had to stop. "He's just a friend," she said.

Tristan snorted. "Right. I've heard that before."

"It's true," she protested. "I've known him all my life, but that's it. We're just friends."

"If you say so. But does Ernesto know that?"

"Of course."

"Are you sure?"

Marlena bit her lip. She hadn't really done much to discourage Ernesto, in fact, she'd done the opposite, in hopes of getting her own way. But standing here, looking into

Tristan's clear blue gaze that telegraphed something much more than friendship, she knew she didn't need to do that anymore. "Yes, I'm sure."

Tristan reached out and brushed her chin with his thumb, sending more shivers up her spine. As he moved closer, her breasts brushed against his hard chest, causing them to tingle. His forefinger slipped under her chin and tilted her face upward. "There's something else I came for," he murmured, and before she knew it, his lips were on hers, warm and soft and insistent. She'd never been kissed before, and never expected it to feel as wonderful as this; the pressure of his mouth against hers, firm and purposeful and without hesitation. It demanded a response, and she gave it to him intuitively. Her lips parted, beckoning him inward. The tip of his tongue slid across her upper lip as she did so, sending yet another quivering thrill rocketing through her body. And she wanted more—more of this dizzy feeling, like standing too close to the edge of a cliff, terrified of falling yet unable to step away.

His arms went around her waist, bringing them closer still. Marlena felt each bump and curve of his muscled body as it fitted against her own soft one. The tingle in her breasts spread downward, lighting up every part of her in its path to the apex between her legs. Her private muscles twitched and her lips moved hungrily against his, liking the lingering flavor of beer in his mouth. She'd never been drunk, but thought this must be what it felt like, her head spinning as though looking down from a great height above the ground—even above the clouds.

"Marly!"

The anguished voice cut through the heady mist of her awakening desires. Abruptly, Tristan released his hold on her and stepped back, breaking the magic kiss. Her head still reeling, she turned to the sound, and felt her heart drop to her toes. "Ernesto…"

"What do you think you're doing," he growled, moving toward them, his dark eyebrows dipping below the rims of his eyeglasses in a murderous scowl. "Get your hands off her!" he demanded, pointing at Tristan, whose hands still rested on her hips.

"Let me go," Marlena whispered.

"Why?" Tristan answered. "Because he wants me to?"

"Because I want you to!"

"Alright," he said, dropping his hands. "But I don't think that's really what you want."

"Marly," Ernesto said, grabbing her arm. "Come on, I'm taking you home."

"I don't want to go home," she argued. "The corrida is not over."

"It is for you and me," he snapped, yanking her toward him. He glared at Tristan. "And for you, senor. Everything's over."

Marlena looked at Ernesto in shock, then back at Tristan, her eyes wide. "I'm sorry," she said, uncertain as to whom she was apologizing; to Tristan? Ernesto? Maybe both. And maybe herself. She closed her eyes against the vision of Tristan standing there staring after them, his silhouette, and her chances, shrinking as Ernesto led her away.

Mierda! What had she done? Now they both hated her, and hated each other even more. With burning hot tears forming behind her eyelids, she realized she hated herself most of all.

Chapter Ten

Marlena shoved open the truck's door and jumped out even before it had come to a standstill in the driveway of her family's villa. "Marly!" Ernesto cried in alarm. "Are you crazy? You could hurt yourself!"

She didn't care. She ran to the house, scampered up the steps and disappeared inside before he could say another word. How dare he treat her like that, as if she were property! He'd embarrassed her and on top of that, been rude to someone he barely knew. More than rude, he'd been downright hostile. Ernesto—hostile! She'd never have believed it of him.

She refused to even speak to him on the ride home. At first he remained angry, demanding to know what she thought she was doing, sneaking around and kissing strangers. But her icy silence soon changed his attitude to one of apology, as he tried to earn her forgiveness. She wouldn't do it. She had a right to do as she pleased, like who she pleased; she didn't plan to hurt her best friend but if changing her future meant doing that, so be it. Ernesto would never change. He'd be stuck on the farm forever.

Flinging herself onto her bed, she re-lived the last moments at the bullring, before Ernesto found them together. Tristan's kiss had awakened something inside her, something deep and powerful and wicked. She liked his strong arms around her, the touch of his lips, and the strange, yet breathtaking sensations he aroused in her own body. The tightening of her nipples and the tingling in her legs and tummy were new and exciting to her, and she wanted more of it. Was that wrong? Was that sinful? Her mother might think so; and there was no way she was going to speak of this to her mother. But she had so many questions, and needed so many answers. Who could she turn to?

Burying her face in her pillow, it came to her. Tía Juliana. She could talk to her aunt; they'd grown a special bond in the months Marlena had taken care of her, and their secret conversations had always been exactly that—secret. Besides, Juliana had been out in the world, chasing her dream, though it had nearly cost her life; and more than that—she knew much about men. Yes, she would talk to her tía.

It would be supper time soon, and her aunt would be awake and waiting to be readied for her meal. Marlena slipped noiselessly down the hall to Juliana's room and knocked softly. Her aunt's low-timbred voice beckoned her to enter. "Pasa." Opening the door, she saw Juliana sitting up in bed, attempting to apply nail polish with her unsteady hands. Baby Jorge slept blissfully in his nearby cradle.

"Let me do that for you, Tía," Marlena said, quickly reaching her aunt's side and sitting on the edge of the bed. She took the bottle of polish and placing Juliana's hand on her lap, took over the job of painting her nails.

"Gracias, cariña."

"You're welcome, Tía; you know that. Anything you need."

Juliana gave a slow nod, her bright eyes fixed on her niece. "And what is it you need, little one?"

Marlena looked up to meet her aunt's gaze. "What makes you think I need something?" Juliana chuckled once more, and it made Marlena happy to see her tía's spirits, and her health, lifting day by day.

"You didn't come to see me just to paint my nails, and it's not yet supper time. You're here for a reason, now what is it?"

Marlena let out a sigh of relief, amazed at her aunt's uncanny insight. She had been right to come to her, seek her advice. "Clever Tía," she said, a warm smile on her face. "You know things about me before I even do." Juliana waited for her to continue speaking. "I need your advice," Marlena began. "I…like someone. Someone I've met. And I kissed him, at the bullfight today."

"Your first kiss?" Juliana asked, although it wasn't really a question. "And what did you think of it?"

Now, there was a question she hadn't expected, but glad for the chance to let all her swirling emotions tumbling out; and she knew she could trust her Tía to keep it between them. Marlena capped the bottle of polish and set it aside. "Oh, Tía…I…I've never felt anything like it…I felt swept away… on top of the world; like nothing else existed but us. There were butterflies in my stomach...and other places." Marlena paused, looking to her aunt for understanding. "Is it wrong to feel like that?"

Juliana shook her head. "No. If it is the right man, it is exactly right. Understand something, cariña; something that your mother nor any other woman in this house will probably ever tell you." She leaned forward. "There is no feeling that compares to being with a man, a man you want. It's not wrong, not shameful. It's wonderful, and it's natural. Remember that."

Marlena nodded, relieved but also surprised by her aunt's revelation. She smiled and felt a blush rise to her cheeks. "I thought it was wonderful too, but now I'm not so sure. I kissed him in front of Ernesto…I didn't mean to, but…suddenly he was just there, watching me. Watching us."

"So?"

"So! They got in a fight, and Ernesto dragged me away like an unruly child. I was so embarrassed. I thought he was my best friend…but it's all going wrong. He's different now. He likes me as more than a friend."

Juliana nodded her understanding. "And you don't feel the same way. But you do for this other person. You don't have to tell me who it is," she added.

"But I want to. I need to."

"No, I meant I already know who it is. It's the Welshman, isn't it? Senor Flynn."

Marlena's mouth dropped open, but she should have known her tía would figure it out. "How did you know that?"

"I told you before, he would bring great change to this house. And there would be a price to pay for it."

"I know, but what did that mean, Tía? You never really said. Tell me now, I need to know. Know what you know; know what I should do."

Juliana lifted her hands to display her burn-scarred skin, her fingernails shining with fresh, copper-red polish. "I'm a poor person to ask about the right thing to do. But I followed my heart, my passions, as everyone should. As you should. No matter the price."

Marlena heaved an exasperated sigh. "But it's not as easy as that, is it? You had to run away to follow your dreams. Are you saying I should do the same?"

"No, child. Things are different now than when I was your age. You have choices. And if you choose to involve Tristan, understand that it is yours alone, and that every choice has consequences."

Marlena's ears alerted. She called him Tristan; not Senor Flynn or The Welshman. She must know more about him than she let on. "Then tell me about him, Tía. Is he a good person? Can I trust him?" She longed to hear the truth of the incident that had been kept locked away all these months.

Juliana drew a long breath and cast a loving gaze over her sleeping baby. A smile tugged at the tight, still-healing skin around her mouth. "I first saw him in a cantina, in Madrid. A tiny, lawless place, but they let me dance, so I worked there for a few pesetas a night, plus whatever the customers gave me in tips." She turned her attention back to her niece. "He was with another man, a loud, brash and arrogant man. Whom I found fascinating. And handsome."

Marlena smiled. "Very handsome?"

"Si, muy handsome. But he became very drunk, shouting and showing off his money. He gave me a big tip to dance at his table."

"And did you?"

"Por supuesto. The cantina owner would have been furious if I didn't. Not good for business. So, I danced. Not a flamenco, like I did for the whole house, but a slow, private dance. A provocative dance." Juliana leaned forward a little, and winked. "I shouldn't tell you this, but I liked doing that kind of dancing. Lifting the ruffles of my skirt, showing off my legs; moving my body to the music in whatever way I wanted. I felt free."

Marlena's eyes widened. "Then what happened?"

"Like most drunken men," she scoffed. "He tried to grab me, touch my behind and pull me into his lap. The thing is, I was attracted to him. I would have sat on his lap willingly if he hadn't been so out of control."

"But you didn't," Marlena concluded. "Did he get angry?"

"He was so drunk I couldn't tell. But I know who was angry. Enzo, the big gypsy man who drank there often. He liked me, and was jealous. I left the dance floor, as the owner told me to do when customers got too friendly. I went outside to get some air, and the drunk man followed me. Enzo was waiting for him, there in the alley. They fought; I watched from the doorway, until Senor Flynn came around from the street and broke it up. Led his friend away."

"That's it?" Marlena asked, disappointed if that was the end of the story. It didn't explain much about Tristan, or the stranger she found so handsome. "But you met them again, yes?"

"Not for a few months. But I didn't want to work at the cantina anymore, because of Enzo. Before all the trouble started, I overheard them talking about a place called El Mirador, on the sea coast, where they were going to make a lot of money. So, one day I went to the coast, and found El Mirador, a fancy hotel. They ran the place. They were hiring dancers, and gave me a job. It was my dream come true, until…" Juliana stopped speaking, and looked again at Jorge, who began to stir and fuss.

"I'll get him," Marlena said, not wanting a crying baby to interrupt the story. She had to hear more. She lifted the squirming bundle from the cradle and brought him to his mother. Juliana took the baby in her arms and held him close. "Until what, Tía?" Marlena prompted.

"Until it burned down," she answered, her throaty voice catching. She looked up with tear-filled eyes. "He saved me you know. And Jorge." She stroked the fine skin of the boy's face with a gentle finger. "By the grace of God my son was spared, allowed to be born, because of Tristan Flynn. He rescued me from the fire, and brought me home; he did not have to do that. That should tell you what kind of man he is."

A man with a conscience, Marlena thought. But that still didn't mean he was conscientious, or trustworthy. It didn't help her to know what to do; and it certainly didn't solve the problem of Ernesto being angry with her. Perhaps Tristan was no longer even interested in her, after what happened today. The thought sent a stab of pain through her heart; a hollow, lost feeling, that he might leave and she'd never see him again. He could go back to his home country and meet another girl. Someone who wasn't bound by tradition or family, who wouldn't act so prissy and immature. Panic rose out of the pain; she didn't want him to leave, and more than anything didn't want him to see him with another woman.

In that moment, she realized she couldn't ignore her feelings for him, sinful or not, and that her future was linked to his. Looking down at her new little cousin also made her remember her promise. That she would provide for him no matter what. Yes, she would follow her heart. And this lion-haired man named Tristan Flynn.

With her mind made up, she helped Juliana dress for supper and change the baby's diapers. But another question remained unasked; and after what Tristan told her that night in the kitchen, Marlena suspected the answer. Was the other man Juliana's lover? Jorge's father? She was dying to know for certain, but couldn't just blurt out such a direct question. Perhaps she could coax it out of her another way. "The drunk man—the handsome one," she asked, as she did up the buttons of her aunt's blouse. "You never said his name. Who was he? Did he at least apologize for his behavior at the cantina?"

"He was not a man who apologized for anything," Juliana said, her voice turning cross. "Especially his actions. Now, don't ask me anymore questions. I am tired and I'm hungry. Let us eat our meal and thank our Lord for the good fortune we have." She raised her palm to Marlena's cheek. "You have the answers you need, child. Act on them."

Chapter Eleven

The blazing sun had nearly disappeared below the horizon as Tristan reached the church yard of the Gracia Immaculata, leaving his clothes dusty and his throat as scorched as the surrounding landscape. It had not been an easy walk from the city's bullring; nor a comfortable one. He did not regret kissing Marlena, in public, in front of hundreds of people. He didn't particularly regret doing so in front of his opponent either; but deeply regretted the scene that followed.

Many eyes turned to them as Ernesto dragged her away through the crowd. While he watched her disappear, Tristan suddenly knew how the mighty bull must have felt when the maddening cape fluttered over his horns. Enraged, and ready to charge; his ego bruised and his temper lost. He could have gone after them, pulled Marlena away and back into his arms, asserting his dominance. But that might have embarrassed her further, and drawn an even bigger circle of onlookers. No, he would choose his battles, and where they would play out; but he had no doubt the battle was looming, and that he would win it.

He already knew the outcome, the moment their lips met. The kiss between he and Marlena had struck fire deep in his belly. The way she opened to him, instinctively and passionately, could not be misinterpreted. He felt the frantic beating of her heart against his chest as he pulled her close, and she brooked no resistance, but—had he overstepped? A young girl feeling her first real pangs of desire might not have had the will to stop herself, or him. He could have exhibited more control; wooed and courted her in what her family probably saw as an appropriate way. But was she really that innocent? Her kiss did not seem tentative or inexperienced. He may be operating from a false assumption. He had no way of knowing what desires, experience or motivations she had, but could not mistake the passion of that kiss. He wanted more, and was determined to have it. Have her.

A surprise greeted him at the back door of the church. The small figure ran to him as he approached. "Ángel," Tristan called out. "What are you doing here? Does Pastor Giorgio know you're here?"

"Si, he knows. He said I could wait for you."

Tristan noted the boy wore the same clothes he had first seen him in. Maybe he had no others. He felt for the kid, never knowing impoverishment himself, but was getting an education in it every day he spent here. "Well, here I am. What's up?"

The boy's brow wrinkled in confusion. "What's…up?"

"Si, uh…que pasa, amigo?" Tristan rephrased in Spanish.

Ángel's eyes lit and a wide smile creased his small, tanned face. "The wheelchair," he said. "Have you finished making it?"

Bloody hell. He'd forgotten all about it. That project still lay in a pile of rubber, spokes and castoff metal parts. "Oh. Ángel, lo siento, I've been a little busy." Ángel's face fell a little, clearly disappointed. He shuffled his bare feet in the dirt. Christ, the kid couldn't even afford shoes. How could Tristan have imagined that building the wheelchair wasn't important, and needed right away? Despite thoughts of Marlena, the blood-soaked bullfight, and the possibility of a trip to Madrid, he vowed to make his promise to Ángel a priority. "But you know, it's almost finished," he lied. "I just need a few more days."

"Can I see it?" Ángel asked, excited.

"Oh…no, not yet. I don't want anyone to see it until it's ready, and until I've tested it for safety."

"Do you think you can be finished by tomorrow?"

"That's a little soon."

"But my mother wants to invite you for dinner tomorrow. You could bring the chair with you."

Tristan felt reluctant to accept the offer of a meal from a family that couldn't even afford footwear. It certainly wouldn't be a lavish spread like he'd had at Casa Sanchez. He didn't quite know what to expect. Did the boy have brothers, sisters? All of them needing to be fed as well? And what about a father—that could be awkward. "Please thank your mother for the invitation," he said. "But Don Giorgio needs me here tomorrow. Perhaps another day."

"Which day?" Ángel pressed.

Tristan laughed and tousled the boy's dark hair. "Why don't you come by on Wednesday. The chair will be ready, I promise."

"Okay," Ángel said, dodging away from his reach. "Miercoles. I'll come back then."

"Miercoles," Tristan repeated, imitating the boy's pronunciation. "That means Wednesday?"

"Don't you know the days of the week? You're not a very fast learner."

"I need a fast teacher. What are the other days then?"

"Lunes, Martes, Miércoles, Jueves, Viernes, Sábado, Domingo," the boy yelled as he dashed away. "Adios, El Milagro!"

The Miracle, Tristan scoffed inwardly. It would take a miracle to construct a wheelchair from old bicycle parts by Wednesday, but he would try. Exhausted, he sighed and stepped inside the building. It might take another miracle for him to see Marlena again. It was a good bet that Ernesto wouldn't be bringing her around; but he couldn't just leave things the way they were. He would have to go to her. See for himself if she cared for him, or was only teasing him to get a rise out of Ernesto. In any case, he'd committed his next few days to the wheelchair project. A visit to the Sanchez villa would have to wait.

*

Despite the magazine being flattened beneath her mattress each time she closed it, its pages naturally fell open to the center, the double page spread unfolding in all its glory and revealing the familiar hazy background and delicious pink satin beneath the beautiful blond woman in the photograph. She lay on her side, leaning up on one elbow, her legs slightly bent and one overlapping the other. Her breasts were large, and her hands cupped them firmly through the thin material of the baby-doll nightgown she wore, thrusting them forward so that the dark circles of her nipples were clearly visible.

Sitting on her bed with the magazine, Marlena's own breasts began to tingle as she gazed at the photo, even though she'd viewed it hundreds of times. Today was different; everything was different, since she'd kissed Tristan at the bullring. Sensations she'd never before experienced flooded her body with frightening speed, though they were not at all frightening in and of themselves. They were exciting, pleasurable, and urgent. Aunt Juliana said it was perfectly natural.

She looked down at her own breasts, disappointed they were not nearly the size of the model's in the magazine. She'd heard there were operations to make them larger, but had no idea how it was done. Dropping the book, her hands went to them, rubbing over her excited nipples, surprised at how they swelled and protruded through the fabric of her shirt the more she touched them, the tingling tightness becoming sweetly painful. She cupped their fullness in her palms and lifted them forward and up, as the woman in the picture did. She closed her eyes and imagined a camera in front of her, tilting her head toward the ceiling so that her long hair trailed down her back. It was one thing in the privacy of her own bedroom, but could she do this in front of a camera man? If she wanted to become a famous model she would have to, she reasoned.

Again, the urgent throbbing in her breasts spread downward, reaching between her legs and causing her private muscles to pulse and twitch. What did that mean? Was that normal, too? When would it stop? What if it didn't? Strangely, her body called to her, begging her to go further, urge the wicked sensations onward. Imagining a camera man watching heightened the urgency, and she could not stop herself.

Rolling over onto her back, she reached below her skirt and placed her hand over her throbbing mound, finding the material of her panties moist. She pressed down, hoping to stem the strange ache, make it go away, but it did not. Instead, it grew in strength, seeming both hot and cold at once, making her feel as if she was sinking into her bed. She applied more pressure, as though to force it back inside her, but her body seemed paralyzed, ceasing to operate in favor of this new thing, this wave of something that now exploded in her core, spilling in every direction like ocean surf cresting against the beach.

It was powerful, unstoppable; a feeling of pleasure and euphoria overtaking her so completely that nothing else mattered, nothing else existed. Indescribable joy cascaded over her, gradually lessening until it stopped altogether. When it was over, Marlena lay quietly, panting for breath, trying to understand what had just happened. Had she been possessed? All the Catholic dogma she'd been taught came rushing into her mind, the evils of sin, of el Diablo and other demons always vying for one's soul. Temptation. It was the tool of such vile entities, and she had succumbed to it, been unable to resist it.

But it had felt so good. How could it be bad? Wouldn't God want everyone want to feel like that? Such ecstasy must surely be as if one were in the presence of God himself. She sat up, retrieving the magazine from where it had fallen on the flcor and tucking it safely away again. There were many things still unknown, ideas so confusing and conflicting that Marlena had more questions than ever. But who could she ask now, about this? Even her tía might not want to speak of it in such detail. She had felt these things when Tristan touched her. Were they warnings? Telling her to stay away, or to get closer? There would be a price, Juliana had said. She hoped that price would not be her eternal soul.

She was not even certain she would see Tristan again. Ernesto had as good as insulted him. He had no reason at all to come to her villa now; and she had no way to get to the church on her own, unless she walked. And what of their promised trip to Madrid? Just hours ago it had seemed all but a matter of choosing a day, when Tristan showed her the old van he'd bought. But now, everything might have changed. Besides, her mother would never allow it, her daughter riding off with a foreign stranger, no matter how highly Bianca thought of him. She'd have to sneak away somehow, and soon.

From her bureau drawer she took out the faded, folded scrap of newspaper she'd carefully preserved, and re-read the magical, tantalizing advertisement:

Models wanted immediately.

No experience necessary - free training provided.

To audition apply in person.

Perhaps the auditions were closed by now—the newspaper being weeks old; but if she didn't try, she would never know, and there was only one way to find out. She'd told her aunt she would brave anything, even fire, to get what she wanted, with or without anyone's help. She would get to Madrid somehow, even if she had to hitch-hike.

Chapter Twelve

"You've been working very hard on this," Don Giorgio said, looking over Tristan's work. "But it seems an unusual thing to build. Wherever did you get the idea, and find the necessary materials?"

Tristan spun the wheels on the chair that sat upturned on a makeshift workbench. They moved freely and without much noise. Satisfied, he set the chair upright and lowered it to the ground. "The idea wasn't mine," he said, "but I like a challenge. And you can find most anything if you know where to look."

"Aieee, es verdad, about much in life," Don Giorgio answered, nodding. "Seek, and ye shall find, no?"

"Si." He smiled at the portly Pastor, then gestured to the chair. "Care to take it for a spin?"

Don Giorgio laughed. "I don't drive."

"Perfect. I'll drive. It needs a road test in any case. Por favor," Tristan said, inviting him to take a seat. "I'll go slow."

With an amused shrug, the clergyman turned and lowered his wide frame into the chair. "Vamonos!"

Tristan grasped the handlebars attached to the chair's back, fashioned from a castoff bicycle, and pushed forward. The man's weight required an extra nudge to get it moving, but move it did, and even better than expected. The wide tires rolled smoothly over the uneven ground of the church yard, their low inflation absorbing the contours of various pebbles, stones and thatches of grass in their path. "Ah, now this is the way to get around," Don Giorgio said. "You may never get me out of this chair, my friend."

"Lo siento, but I'm afraid you will have to, Padre. Here comes my client now." Tristan pointed to the church yard gate as Ángel's slight figure scurried up to it.

"Ha ha, El Milagro! I knew you could do it!" the boy exclaimed with a gleaming, toothy smile. He unlatched the gate and strode in. "My mother is going to love it! She will love you, senor!"

Don Giorgio rose from the chair as they came to a halt, turning a curious eye toward Tristan. "Indeed? It is for Senora Ibanez?"

Tristan never actually heard Ángel's surname, but of course the Pastor would know everyone in town, and especially within his congregation. He nodded in affirmation. "My client is very persuasive and insistent. He held me to a deadline."

"I see. And what price did you agree on?" Don Giorgio asked the boy good-naturedly.

Ángel's smile broadened. "He is coming to our house for supper."

"Muy bien. I'm sure—Senor Milagro—could use a fine meal, cooked by a fine hand, rather than mine," the Pastor concluded. "It's been awhile since she has had company to entertain, being a young widow," he added, clearly for Tristan's ears. "And a fine teacher, as well. You can learn your Spanish from her very quickly. A fine trade for such fine work. I'm proud of you, mi hijo." Tristan frowned at the Pastor's amused expression and thinly veiled hint.

Ángel ran his small brown hand over the chair's frame. "You will make my mother very happy. Can we take it now?"

"You go ahead and take it, Ángel. I have other things to do right now," Tristan said.

"But you have to come with me. Supper's almost ready!" he exclaimed.

Tristan held up his hands. "I didn't say I would come for supper, remember? I only said to come for the chair today." The boy looked nearly heartbroken. As Don Giorgio folded his hands across his ample belly and glanced between the two of them, Tristan began to smell a setup. "I don't want to intrude," he added.

"Oh, I'm sure you wouldn't be intruding," Don Giorgio declared. "If Senora Ibanez is expecting you, it would be rude to turn down the invitation. Besides, a young man like you needs to…" he paused, looking him up and down, a wry grin on his face. "…be nourished, no?"

Tristan did not miss the intimation of what young men needed, and the last thing he wanted to do was to disappoint anyone, least of all his employer; but he wasn't interested in whatever the good pastor thought Ángel's mother could offer. "Alright, Ángel," he sighed, flashing a resigned smile. "Lead the way."

With a goodbye wave to Don Giorgio, Ángel grasped the chair's handles and steered it through the gate and around to the front street. "Let me know when you get tired," Tristan said.

"Oh, I not tired, senor. I not old like you."

"Who are you calling old, pipsqueak," Tristan laughed.

"Pip…skw…" Ángel faltered over the unfamiliar moniker. "That better not be a bad word."

"Not as bad as old. Just how old do you think I am?"

"Old enough."

"For what?"

Ángel grinned sideways at him and moved ahead of Tristan, pushing the chair forward in an extra burst of youthful enthusiasm. Tristan widened his stride in response. "Oh, don't even think it, pipsqueak; I can leg it better than most old men."

The boy laughed and sped up, only to come to a hard stop at the end of the block. When Tristan caught up, he followed Ángel's gaze to the center of the cobbled square that lay just ahead. A ring of townsfolk encircled the massive trunk of El Guardián, its bark now nearly completely stripped, exposing a dry and graying cambium beneath, a sure sign of the tree's declining health.

"What are they doing?" Ángel asked, observing as the group talked among themselves, and some men measured the tree's girth with a tape. "Make them get away from it," he scowled.

"Maybe they're trying to help it," Tristan offered, sensing the boy's anxiety. Flaming hell. Among all the other things he'd forgotten or ignored lately, El Guardián had been one of them. His plan to divert the well water to the tree via underground pipe had gone completely by the wayside in his fixation over a certain pretty brunette and her omnipresent boyfriend. He could do it, he was sure, but it might already be too late, judging not only by the sickly look of the tree, but by the clear intentions of the men around it. They were making preparations to cut it down.

Ironically, that was exactly what he'd thought to do, the day he'd nearly crashed into it. Now, the idea seemed abhorrent and brutal. He had to intervene. "Wait here," Tristan said to a nervous Ángel, and strode across the square. He could hear many voices all speaking at the same time, much too rapidly and jumbled together to be intelligible to him, but what he saw spoke louder than any words. Toolboxes filled with hand saws, axes and rope. An open tailgate on a nearby pickup, ready to receive the aftermath of the task they appeared ready to perform. "Que pasa," he whispered to one of the onlookers near him. "What are they trying to do?"

The man turned to him. "What does it look like?"

"They plan to cut it down? I thought everyone wanted the tree saved."

The man shook his head. "Si, but those men say it cannot be saved. Some believe that, others do not."

Tristan's brain raced, thinking of all that Ángel had told him. If the tree held as much spiritual value as the little well did, they couldn't just hack it down like this. It may still have life in its roots. He needed time; time to put his design into action, and to put a stop to this ham-handed way the workers planned to execute their task. "You can't do it with those tools." he shouted.

Heads turned to the sound of his voice. "Pardoneme, senor?" one of the workmen said.

"You'll never get through the size of that trunk with those. And safety precautions must be taken, so that no one is injured. This is a public place, there are rules."

"How would you know these rules, senor? You're not from Zaragoza."

"No, but I am an engineer; and there's a better way to deal with this. A proper way."

"It's a tree. How many ways are there," another workman scoffed, brandishing his ax in demonstration. Expressions of outrage rippled through the crowd.

"We can save it," Tristan called out. "I can save it."

The crowd quieted as he spoke. "Indeed, senor. And who are you?" the first workman asked.

"He is El Milagro," a voice rang out, much larger than the person it belonged to. Ángel stood at the back of the group, still gripping the wheelchair's handlebars. "He can do anything. He built this wheelchair for my mother. He fixed the well. He can save El Guardián."

More voices rose from within the growing crowd. "Milagro?" muttered some. "Impossible!" cried a few. "Let him try," said others. The workman shouted over the din. "We have orders from the city council to remove it by the end of the week, senor."

"Then let me speak to the council," Tristan said. "If they disagree with what I have to say, then by all means, swing your axes." The gathered townsfolk clapped and whistled their approval. "Do we have a deal?"

With a nod from the head workman, the others began to pack up their tools. "The council may not have time to see you today," he warned. "But I can direct you to the town hall."

"I'll take my chances," Tristan answered, and made his way through the crowd toward Ángel. The boy looked sad, but awestruck at the same time. "I'm sorry Ángel, but I think you'll have to go on home without me. I have to get to the town hall as soon as possible."

Ángel nodded. "I knew you would stop them," he said. "I'll tell my mother you were too busy saving El Guardián to come to supper." He maneuvered the chair away from the crowd and back onto the sidewalk. As he walked away, he looked back over his shoulder and flashed a broad smile. "She will love you even better!"

Folding his arms, Tristan watched the boy move down the street while he waited for the men to escort him to the town hall. Now he was certain a plot was afoot; to somehow hook him up, to spark some romantic interest in him for Senora Ibanez. A widow, huh? That explained a lot. Don Giorgio was very forthcoming with that information. He recalled Ángel's mother being pretty enough, even as she leaned on her cane at the well ceremony. He felt pity for her, but these two unlikely matchmakers would be very disappointed. His romantic interests were already sparked, bursting into flame, and building to an inferno in his very soul.

Committing to yet another 'miracle' project would further keep him away from the source of that fire; but he couldn't back out now. He had to put his money where his big, egotistical mouth was; though he'd much rather be putting his mouth on the soft lips of Marlena Sanchez…and every other part of her body. He wiped his brow as he trudged to the town hall under the searing heat of the sun. This country had taken hold of him in ways he'd never imagined since that crazy night with Ariel at the cantina; and apparently it wasn't about to let him go.

Chapter Thirteen

"Pencils down."

Marlena did as her teacher commanded, breathing a long-awaited sigh of relief as she slapped the yellow wooden stick to the desktop with the flat of her palm. Finally. It was done. The last exam she'd ever write inside this school building. She was free.

Turning in her test paper felt like a weight off her shoulders. One less obstacle between her and her dream. But how to make the dream a reality? The days since the bullfight brought nothing but uncertainty. Tristan had not returned to the villa to seek her out; and though Ernesto had come to finish the pig barn, she carefully avoided having to speak to him.

Today however, she'd not be so lucky. There he stood by her locker, waiting for her, just as he did every day at the bus stop. For that reason, she'd purposely chosen a seat away from him on the bus, and today, opted to walk to school. She pictured him waiting for the bus this morning, pacing and looking about, wondering where she could be. Marlena sighed. Now was as good a time as any to cut the apron strings between them; even if it meant slashing the very fibers of her friend's heart.

He turned toward her, one nervous finger pushing his dark-rimmed glasses up the bridge of his nose. "Marly!" he called.

"Hi," she answered without inflection. She opened her locker and pretended to rummage through it, though she'd emptied it of its contents days ago. Only one item remained. The packed traveling bag she'd hidden there this morning. Ernesto mustn't see it.

"Are you not even going to talk to me?" he asked, breaking the icy silence.

"Why should I?" she answered, shielding herself with the locker door. "You've made your position clear. You expect to own me; push me around like a bad child. I already have parents. I don't need you acting like one."

"I'm trying to apologize," he said. "I've been apologizing all week. Can't you even listen to me for one minute?"

"Apologize all you like, but I'm leaving. Get it through your head. You and I have no future."

"Don't say that," Ernesto replied, his voice choked with denial. "We have our whole lives ahead of us. Everything can change."

Marlena turned, finally looking her childhood friend straight in the eyes. "You can do what you love best, which is to stay here forever, but I'll be going to Madrid. And yes, everything will change. It already has."

Ernesto looked back at her as though she had two heads, his mouth gaping open in disbelief. "It's like I don't know you anymore," he said, shaking his head. "Who you are. You're not the Marly I grew up with."

"That's just it," she said, exasperation in her voice. "We're all grown up now, Ernesto, both of us. We're not children any longer, and I am who I am. Who I'm going to be."

Ernesto's square, stern jaw worked back and forth, grinding up his next words like grain in a flour mill. "It's because of him, isn't it? That Flynn. What's he done to you?"

"Nothing," she answered. It was only partly a lie. "Except to show me that a different kind of life is possible."

"Don't listen to him Marly. He'll hurt you. He's not right for you."

"And you are?" she rounded on him. "Embarrassing me in front of all those people? Telling me what to do?"

"I'm only trying to protect you."

Marlena shook her head. This conversation was going nowhere; the argument pointless and unnecessary. It would only leave bad feelings between them forever. She didn't want it to end that way, knowing the possibility that she might never see him again. Her voice softened. "I know that. Because you care for me. I care for you, too, Ernesto; I do. I just don't need protection. I don't need you."

The look of hurt on the sweet face she'd known all her life stabbed at her heart, but she couldn't take back the words. She meant them.

"Then what do you need, Marly? Tristan? A foreigner who can't possibly understand you, or our way of life? You don't know him, or what he's capable of. He's practically a stranger."

"I didn't say I wanted him. I want the kind of freedom he has. Anyway, I don't have to answer to you, or anyone else."

"Not even your mother? Does she know you're planning to leave?"

"That's none of your business." Marlena hadn't broached the topic of leaving, or any topic really, with Bianca, aside from telling her she would be going shopping after school today. She felt guilty lying to her mother, but it was too late for regrets. The bag hidden in her locker held clothes, makeup, and money for bus fare. No one could stop her now. She was leaving directly from school. Ernesto didn't need to know that. "Right now, it's you who needs to leave. As in leave me alone. I want to clean my locker."

Ernesto backed away from where they stood. "Fine," he said coldly. "If that's how you want it. Have a nice life. But when it doesn't work out, don't expect any help from me."

She watched him walk away, his back straight and his shoulders squared atop his slim frame. He didn't look back. And neither would she. When he was out of sight, she grabbed her bag and slammed the bent and pitted locker door, along with her childhood life, shut with a bang.

*

Digging the trench was a slow process. The water table beneath the well became significantly lower the closer they got to the town square; too deep to dig a direct line to it with the manual tools at Tristan's disposal. But with enough pipe and fittings scrounged from various suppliers he would be able to connect the wellspring to El Guardián. However, it meant burying the pipe underground, to ensure a downward flow and to protect it from traffic damage.

With each strike of his shovel, Ángel worked alongside him scooping away the dislodged earth with a bucket. "This hard work," the boy exclaimed between scoops. "But it bring life to El Guardián, yes?"

"It should," Tristan said. "You see, the vitality…la vida… of any plant or tree is in its roots, not its leaves. That is, what's below the ground is more important than what's above."

Ángel laughed and nodded. "Like people. What is underneath is who they really are. Not what they say or how they look."

"Exactemente," Tristan said, straightening from his bent-over stance to mop the sweat from his face with a well-used red bandanna he kept in his back pocket. The kid was perceptive beyond his years. He could not help but apply the observation to the object of his affection. Marlena Sanchez kept a cool surface, but Tristan felt certain her blood ran hot beneath the smooth, fair skin. Her kiss was proof of that, and he wanted to bring it to boil, have it spill over with passion, even if it burned him in the process. And he couldn't do that from the business end of a shovel. He plunged the implement into the ground with renewed force, determined to get the job done as soon as possible.

"I think that is true of you, Senor," Ángel continued. "You don't talk about yourself. You are mysterioso."

"There's no mystery to me," Tristan laughed. "I'm a penniless student doing the classic student thing; trekking across Europe just for the experience. See new countries, meet new people."

Ángel kept at his task for a moment before speaking again. "How come you not married?" he asked suddenly.

"Oh, I'm not ready for that," Tristan scoffed. "I have nothing to offer a wife. No job, no home. And I'm way too young."

"You old enough," Ángel replied.

"Yeah, so you've said. You think I'm a crippled old man," Tristan reminded him. "Besides, I haven't met the right woman yet."

"But you've met lots of women here. Every woman wants to get married," Ángel said.

"Is that so? Like who?" Tristan's thoughts again focused on Marlena, even as the words left his lips. His attraction to her felt irresistible, indecently so; but marriage? Christ, she was only eighteen. She'd never left home, or her family. Did she dream of marriage? If he continued his pursuit of her, surely marriage would be expected. He'd better re-think his intentions and cool his randy jets before things got out of hand. But that would be like throwing a pitcher of water at a raging fire. He might slow it down, but would never quench it. The vision of her nude body sprawled beneath him in a moment of passionate lovemaking resurfaced in his mind more often than he wanted to admit.

Ángel kept his head down, continuing to scrape away the mounds of sandy soil with his bucket. "Like my mother," he said. "She needs a husband."

Tristan jabbed at a fresh patch of dirt with his shovel, ramming it into the earth with all his might. Ángel's statement answered a lot of questions, except the obvious. "She is not married to your father?"

"He died. A long time ago." Ángel cast a shy glance upward. "You would make a good husband for her."

Tristan paused and leaned on the handle of his shovel, returning the boy's expectant gaze. How to tell a ten-year-old he had no interest in his mother, without hurting his feelings? "I'll take that as a compliment," Tristan said. "But like I said, I'm not ready for anything like that."

Ángel's lips pouted in thought. "When you think you be ready?"

Tristan had to laugh at Ángel's persistence. "Not for a long time." He crouched down to the boy's level. "Listen, Ángel. I like you. And I'm flattered that you think of me as good husband material, but I have many things to do yet with my life. Things to accomplish."

"Like what?"

"Like this pipe, for one. And other things…big things. Like buildings and bridges." Tristan smiled and slapped Ángel lightly on his arm before rising to his feet again. "So, c'mon, let's get back to work. Trabajo!"

"After that you get married?" Ángel asked hopefully. "That sounds like a long time. You really be old by then. Maybe no woman want you."

Tristan laughed again. "Maybe so. But at least I'll be able to afford a wife, even if I don't get one." The idea of marrying Marlena floated perniciously in his mind. And then he remembered Ernesto. Did his designs on Marlena extend to marriage? Were they already lovers? He didn't appear to be much older than she. Perhaps it was just puppy love, that would fade over time; but perhaps it wouldn't. It might grow and mature and…his line of thought cut off and headed in a new direction. Would he be able to go off and build his dreams, and expect the girl to still be here? Still waiting? With his rival still in the wings? Hardly. He'd be damned if he let someone else have her. He would have to come to terms with his feelings for her; and if his desire ran as deep as his fantasies, the time to make a move was sooner rather than later.

Soon, Tristan's shovel struck something hard. The roots of El Guardián! He looked up, noting they were perhaps thirty feet from the tree's dying, brittle trunk. The root system had grown massive, seeking the ever-scarcer life-giving nourishment from the earth. He dug deeper and faster, creating a sloping channel in which to lay the last section of pipe that would deliver the needed water right to the giant, subterranean heart of El Guardián.

Tristan and Ángel backtracked several yards to the previous section of pipe they'd completed, which he'd closed off with a valve made from a garden tap. Sweating but spurred on by the prospect of finishing the task, Tristan laid the last piece of pipe into the trench and connected it, a rusty hose clamp having to serve as a flange. It would leak, but any escaping moisture would filter into the surrounding ground, which would only help other vegetation along the way. Breathless from heat and exertion, he turned the valve and rose to his feet.

"What now?" Ángel asked.

"We wait for the flow to build up. Let's go see," Tristan said, practically running to the open end of the pipe they'd just laid. Ángel scampered close behind. Peering into the open trench, he saw the soil turning dark with moisture around the pipe's opening, and then the formation of a small puddle. Soon, a visible trickle of water emerged from the end of the pipe.

A tired, but grateful smile creased his dust-covered face. He reached out and ruffled Ángel's dark, bedraggled hair on the top of his head. "Muy bien, well done!" he shouted. The boy responded by wrapping his arms around Tristan's waist in a hug. They stood and watched the pool of water grow and deepen for several moments. The pipeline was a success, but the rest was up to El Guardián. It might be months before any new growth would be seen. He'd explained that to the town council when they gave him permission to proceed, as well as how the tree would need severe trimming in order to spur new growth.

But for today, their work was nearly done. Tristan and Ángel backfilled the trench with the displaced earth and returned to where he'd parked the old blue van, tossing their tools into the cargo area in a gesture of triumph. "I think this calls for a celebration," Tristan said as he closed the rear doors of the van. "Want to come along? Maybe get some ice cream?"

Ángel nodded enthusiastically. They climbed into the van and drove to the confectioner's shop where Tristan treated the boy to a triple scoop cone and himself to a cold bottle of beer. "I still wish you would marry my mother," Ángel said between licks of ice cream as they left the shop. "Then I would have a new father, too." The boy looked at Tristan, his dark eyes brimming with undisguised honesty and longing. Tristan stooped to one knee and gripped Ángel by the shoulders.

"Now, that would truly be a milagro," Tristan said. "Someday, you may have a new father, Ángel; but you know, a man doesn't have to marry your mother to be one to you. A father is someone who teaches you, shows you wrong from right, protects you, cares about you; and loves you no matter what."

Ángel considered this as rivulets of melting ice cream dripped over the lip of his cone and onto his small hand. "Do you love me, Milagro?"

"I do, Ángel. I care about you and you can always count on me as long as I'm around."

Ángel smiled. "Then, you are my father," he beamed. "You do all of those things."

Tristan returned the smile, knowing he'd stepped into that one with both feet. But if Ángel thought of him as a father figure, what was the harm? The kid certainly needed one, so why not himself? "You go on home now," he said. "I have to get back to the church. I'll see you tomorrow, okay?"

"Okay," Ángel said, and skipped away with his ice cream, waving a cheerful goodbye with his free hand. Tristan got to his feet and pulled the grimy bandanna from his pocket again. Wiping the caked-on dirt and dust from his face he climbed into the van with the satisfaction of a job well done. It remained to be seen if El Guardián would truly recover; but with roots like that, the tree stood a good chance. No miracles required.

He started the engine and headed toward his own, at least for now, home at the Gracia Immaculata, looking forward to a bath or at least a quick duck under the garden hose outside the church. Turning off the main street, he slammed on the brakes. It couldn't be. A slim but shapely silhouette with long brown locks stood at the bus stop. Tristan nudged the vehicle forward, riding the clutch until he pulled up alongside the girl. She whirled an about-face as his squealing brakes brought him to a full stop, her hair swinging out in a brunette fan as she turned. He loved that hair, his fingers aching to touch its dark silkiness. "Hi," he called through the open passenger window.

"What are you doing here," Marlena asked, her captivating eyes widening in either surprise or fear. Perhaps both.

"I was about to ask you the same thing. Shouldn't you be at school?"

"School is finished," she said, with a regal lift of her chin. "Shouldn't you be at the church?"

Tristan smiled, running a hand through his own hair that must look like a wild blond bush by now in a futile attempt to look presentable. He wished he weren't so filthy and sweaty. He probably smelled like shit, too, but couldn't stop himself from speaking his next words. "Well now, seeing as we're both where we're not supposed to be, can I give you a lift?"

Chapter Fourteen

"I'm going to Madrid," Marlena said. His offer of a lift seemed too little too late. He knew she wanted to go there; they'd talked about and planned it, but he hadn't shown up in days.

"What a coincidence," he said, smiling through the grime on his face. "So am I."

He practically leapt from the driver's seat to open the door for her. He looked tired and sweat-soaked, but still handsome in spite of all that. The magic moments of their kiss came back to her as though they were still happening. Her heart began to pound, and felt heated blood rushing to her face, threatening to burst out in an embarrassing blush of pink.

Her mind spun. The bus would stop at every dusty crossroads from here to Madrid, picking up not only passengers but probably dogs and chickens on the way as well. She would get to the city far sooner driving with him. The open door to the van beckoned like a portal to another dimension; a time machine that could transport her to another world, one she'd craved and dreamed about. She'd come this far; she couldn't go back. It was all or nothing now. Squaring her shoulders, she lifted her bag and stepped as daintily as she could manage into the cab.

Tristan closed her door and sprinted around to the driver's side. "I need to stop at the church first, but we can get on the road right after that," he said, sliding behind the wheel and shifting the vehicle into gear.

A wave of panic swept over her; she hadn't counted on any delays, or the possibility of seeing anyone else she knew before leaving. Least of all the local Pastor who would obviously question them, or worse, report back to her family, whether intentionally or not. On top of that, any extra minutes she spent in her home town were that many minutes to change her mind, or lose her nerve. "Oh. I thought…we could just leave straight from here."

Tristan looked at her, his intense blue eyes seeming to penetrate into her thoughts, her soul. With all that had happened, with everything her tía said, and the way she felt in his presence, she would never be able to keep secrets from him, for all her efforts to distance herself. They were linked in ways she had yet to understand. He would find her out, one way or another.

"I should tell Don Giorgio where I'm going; and I want to get cleaned up," he said, switching his gaze forward and pulling away from the curb. "You're not exactly catching me at my best," he chuckled.

"Then let me out. I'll take the bus," she said, her voice rising in pitch. "I don't want to miss it."

"What's your hurry," Tristan asked, throwing her a sidelong glance. "I only need a few minutes. We'll still get there faster than the bus."

"No. I mean, it's alright. You have other things to do. Please let me out."

"Marly…"

"Don't call me that," she scowled, her fingers wrapped around the door handle. Only one person called her Marly, and she didn't want to think about him, or the fact he'd likely be skulking around her family's villa within the hour, looking for her. She needed to leave. Now. With Tristan or without.

Tristan pulled over. "Isn't that what most people call you? Sorry if that's too familiar, but it's a long drive to Madrid. Don't you think we should drop the formalities?"

"You can call me whatever you want, just not that."

"Why? Because it's your lover's pet name for you?"

Marlena glared at him. "He's not…we're not…" she broke off and shook her head. "I've told you. It's not like that."

"What is it like then, between you two? Because if he's not your lover, he puts on a pretty good imitation of it," Tristan said, a tinge of anger in his voice.

"It doesn't matter. I'm leaving anyway." She pulled on the handle, the rusted door opening with protest. Tristan grabbed her other wrist.

"Then leave with me," he said. "Please don't get out. We'll go now, if that's what it takes to get you away from him." His words were firm, commanding, but she didn't mind it coming from him. It seemed right. She dared to look into his blue gaze once more. His features softened into a smile. "If you can stand the smell."

Only when Marlena pulled the door shut again did he release his hold on her arm. "I'll try," she said, returning a teasing half-smile. She was used to the odor of hard-working men; there were many of them in her mother's employ. It didn't bother her. All that mattered was that she was on her way.

"So, I asked you a question," Tristan said, after pulling back into traffic. "What exactly is your relationship with Ernesto? And don't say it's none of my business."

Marlena sighed. "I've known him a long time. Since I was born, it seems. But things have changed. At least for him."

"So, you are not lovers."

"No!" she practically shouted. That implied she and Ernesto had…she couldn't imagine it. Had sex? It had never occurred to her, and did not really know what sex would be like, but the idea of Tristan thinking she was not a virgin bothered her even more than his bold question. Of course, she was a virgin! Weren't girls in his country virgins at her age? Doubts flooded her mind. Maybe that wasn't normal where he came from; perhaps he'd think her an oddity for being so. This man made her question almost everything about herself; what she knew, how she felt. He unnerved her at the same time he fascinated her. "A gentleman wouldn't ask such questions," she added.

His smile flashed unnaturally bright against the tanned and dirt-tracked skin of his face. The devil's own smile, Marlena thought; but irresistible for all of that. "You'll have to make do with me," he said, glancing out the side window as he made a turn, his obtuse answer clear enough. The idea he didn't consider himself a gentleman sent an alarming thrill up her spine and another bout of familiar buzzing beneath her panties. "If you say you are not lovers, then I believe you," he went on. "I'm glad, actually."

"Why is that."

He took his eyes off the road long enough to train them on her for a full second. "Because I don't think he's right for you."

Marlena laughed. "He said the same thing about you."

"Well, he's wrong." Tristan returned his attention to the road. The city of Zaragoza began to disappear behind them as they drove. "I'm exactly the right man for you."

"How do you know that?"

"I think we both know that. Don't think I didn't notice how you kissed me."

"What can you tell from a kiss? Maybe I kiss every boy like that."

His mouth dropped open for a split second, then he shook his head. "You don't," he argued. "I know you don't. You know you don't."

A blush rose again to her cheeks, and she crossed her arms to hide her nipples as they tingled and tightened beneath her blouse. He knew her. Better than she knew herself, it seemed. Her body had become like an untrained farm animal around him, plainly displaying every urge and stimulus she felt with no warning or control. It couldn't be right. But it wouldn't stop, and she didn't want it to. She was on her way now, to her own life and her own destiny. Why shouldn't her body be as free as her spirit?

They drove on without speaking for a time. When nothing but open hills and plains filled the view all around them, Tristan spoke again. "Are you staying with family in Madrid?" She shook her head no. "Have you booked a room, or an apartment?" Again, she shook her head. His brow wrinkled in concern. "Why are you, I mean we, going then? It will be almost dark when we get there."

"I have an appointment."

"Where? For what?"

"A job."

"Oh. When do you start? It must be soon if you're in such a hurry."

"I haven't got the job yet. I'm going to apply when I get there."

Tristan plied the brakes and brought the van to a stop on the shoulder. "Does your mother know you're going to Madrid?" he asked, turning to her.

"Please," she said, her eyes turning tearful. "This is my only chance. I have to do this. If I don't get there soon, it may be too late."

"Why? Too late for what?"

"There's a company, who will train me and everything. I don't know how much longer they'll be taking applications. Can you just drive, please? I have to get there. I can't go back now."

Tristan looked at her as though alarm bells were sounding off inside his head, but he said nothing. Her tearful, pleading glance seemed to have silenced his objections. There was no turning back for either of them. What lay ahead would involve both of them, possibly for life. "Alright," he said, moving the gear back into first. "We'll go."

*

"This is it," Marlena said, glancing from the torn piece of newsprint in her hand to the in-need-of-repair glass entrance door in the middle of a commercial block of businesses they'd pulled up in front of. Aged and crumbling stucco cladded the exterior, and the darkened windows revealed nothing of what might lay behind.

"Are you sure," Tristan said, sounding unconvinced. "It doesn't look much like a place of business to me. Let me see that ad." He reached for the scrap of paper she held. In a flash, she crumpled it into her palm.

"I'm sure," she said, taking a deep breath to quell the anxiety rising in her chest. She'd come all this way; the last thing she needed was someone to question her decision, or worse, talk her out of it. The place did look empty and a little forbidding, making her mouth go dry despite the perspiration she felt forming on the back of her neck and under her arms. It was only for the interview anyway, she reasoned. The training facility could be somewhere else entirely. And if she was too late, there was nothing she could do about it; but if it wasn't… the ticket to her dreams could lie just a few steps away. There was only one way to find out. She moved to exit the van.

"I don't like it," Tristan muttered. "Something's not right about this. Don't go in there." He grasped her forearm, but Marlena shook free. "At least let me go with you," he pleaded.

"No." if she wasn't accepted, or if the applications were closed, she didn't want him to witness her failure. But it wasn't the only reason. It occurred to her that her whole life she'd been supervised, guided and accompanied in everything by others. Her mother. Her church. Even Ernesto. For once, she was going to do something alone and independently. "I don't need an escort, or a bodyguard," she argued. "Just wait here."

She saw Tristan's stubbled jaw tighten, and his blue eyes take on a leaden hue. "Count on it."

Chapter Fifteen

"I'll leave the doors open," Tristan said. "I might go get us something to drink, so if I'm not here when you come out, just get in the van and wait, okay?"

"Claro," Marlena said, clambering out of her seat. Stepping onto the crumbling concrete curb, she paused. "I don't know how long I'll be."

Tristan shrugged. He'd wait. He didn't want to let her out of his sight; certainly not here, in what looked like a seedy neighborhood. But he had to let her go. "Doesn't matter. I'll be here." With trepidation, he watched her swing open the dingy glass door of the building and disappear into the darkness beyond it. He felt as though the place had swallowed her, that she might never come out. He shook the irrational fear from his mind and looked around. Near the end of the shabby strip of businesses on the block, he saw a launderia that had coin-operated public showers. He wanted to clean himself up more than ever, so he shoved the gear into park and got out of the van. If he hurried, he could be in and out in ten or fifteen minutes.

The launderia was small but bright inside, and thankfully no line-up for the showers at the back of the shop. He fished out enough coins for the shower as well as for a tiny, guest-sized bar of soap from a vending machine on the wall. Preferring not to think too much about who or what might have used the facility before him, he undressed inside the small, humid enclosure. The clink of his coins dropping into the meter immediately launched an almost blistering-hot stream of water from above, but it felt good, nonetheless.

His aching parts were soothed, his muscles eased by the flow of water as he let it cascade down his neck, shoulders and back. He'd liked to have stayed in the comfort of it for an hour, but knew the meter would run out in mere minutes, if not sooner. He soaped up his sweaty skin, his hand lingering over his cock and balls as he spread the suds over them. The image of a naked Marlena sharing the space with him entered his mind, the rising steam not only from the dribbling water, but their passionate exploration of each other. Damn, if he had more coins he'd be tempted to relieve the tension in his awakening cock.

Sitting next to the girl for more than two hours on the road had been both ecstasy and torture at the same time; God, she was beautiful. He didn't want the trip to end. They'd planned to come to Madrid to see museums and architecture, drink in the Spanish culture; now that they were here, it seemed silly to about-face and go all the way back to Zaragoza. Perhaps they could stay the night, find a modest hotel somewhere nearby. Oh my, what would her mother think then?

With a metallic snap, the comforting flow of water came to an abrupt halt and put and end to his runaway thoughts. He dried and dressed quickly. Sadly, fresh clothes were not an option but at least his body felt clean beneath his soiled and smelly threads. By the time he returned to the van, carrying two bottled sodas from a nearby convenience store, dusk shrouded the street. He hoped to see Marlena's silhouette inside the cab as he drew nearer, but those hopes were dashed when the empty passenger seat greeted him. The interview must have gone longer than expected; but from a job-seekers perspective that was usually a good sign.

He climbed into the driver's seat and set the soda bottles on the dash, then turned the ignition on to fiddle with the radio dials in hopes of raising a decent frequency. He hadn't thought to check out whether the radio even worked before he bought the thing. When he finally coaxed some crackly strains of folk music through the speakers, he sat back and surveyed the street. No movement near the door that Marlena had entered, and with a start, he realized the whole place was completely dark inside; no lights on at all. It didn't look right. Didn't feel right.

How long had she been in there? He drummed his fingertips on the wheel, wrestling with his better judgment, the tension in his muscles, acid beginning to swirl in his gut. Glancing down, he noticed a crumpled ball of paper on the floor. He reached for it, realizing Marlena must have dropped it in her hurry to get out. Careful not to tear it, he unraveled the sorry-looking wad and flattened it against the dash.

*

Tristan was beginning to act like Ernesto, Marlena thought; exerting his authority under the guise of concern and protection. Did men in every country do that? If so, it was becoming tiresome. Wasn't being held back by tradition and government bad enough, without every male in sight getting in the way, too? She almost felt relieved to step through the storefront door and leave Tristan's company behind, but still nervous as to what she might find inside.

Her eyes adjusted to the dim, and beneath a slow-moving ceiling fan, an overweight, dark-haired man sat behind a solitary desk. He looked up as she approached, pulling a lit cigarette from between his lips and exhaling smoke. "Sí?" he asked as the foul-smelling wisps rose upward into the fan's circling blades. His dark eyes traveled up and down her height, but seemed to hold no glint of interest toward her. Even so, she felt paralyzed under his steely, apathetic gaze.

"I'm here to answer this ad," she began, but realizing the old news clipping she'd had in her hand was gone; she must have dropped it. She swallowed hard and gathered her courage, lifting her chin and speaking clearly. "About models being needed? And training provided?"

The man stubbed out his cigarette in a tin tray on the desk, adding to a sizeable and disgusting pile of old butts. "We are no longer taking applications for that," he said, his voice deep and gruff. "You should go on home."

Marlena's heart fell. "Oh no," she said aloud. "I know the ad was from weeks ago, but…I couldn't get here until now. Can't you let me audition? Please? I've come a long way, and I know I'd be good at it, if you give me a chance."

He turned in his swivel chair and looked her over once more, his lower lip protruding in a doubtful manner. "How old are you?"

"Eighteen," she said proudly.

"You have ID on you?"

Marlena dove her hand into her traveling bag. "Yes," she said, pulling out a card and handing it to the man. She didn't own a driver's license, but her school ID had her birthdate on it. She looked hopefully at him while he scrutinized the card. When he looked up, his expression seemed more agreeable than before, and his eyes wandered over her again.

"We may have something," he said, gripping the arms of his chair to lift himself to his feet. "If you think you're so good. A moment." He turned down a short hallway that was curtained off at the end. He parted the drape just enough to stick his head through. "You want to look at another one?"

he said, gesturing with his chin back toward where Marlena stood.

"Yeah, sure," came a man's voice from inside.

The man turned around and motioned for her to come. Marlena moved down the hall toward him. He stopped her as she reached the curtain. "You can leave that with me," he said, nodding to her bulky bag. Marlena hesitated. "I'll keep it safe," he assured her. "You won't need it in there."

She didn't want to ruin her chances by being difficult; this could be her big ticket. Surely they weren't going to steal her belongings. She smiled and handed the bag over. The man held the curtain aside.

Marlena passed through the opening into a dimly lit space. It smelled of dust and stale smoke. As her eyes adjusted, she saw electrical cables snaking across the floor and what looked like lighting equipment in the center of a black-draped room. The same male voice echoed from the surrounding darkness. "Well, hurry up. Stand on the mark."

She scurried forward to stand over a crude letter X taped on the floor between the metal light stands. She noticed a camera fastened to another, three-legged stand. "My name is Marlena," she said into the shadows. She sensed movement from off to one side, and with a snapping sound, the little space flooded with light from all sides. On reflex she blinked and shielded her eyes with one hand.

"Yeah, sure," the voice said from behind where the camera stood. "We don't have all day, Marlene. Let's get on with it."

"Marlena," she corrected. He didn't sound very friendly. But maybe he'd had a long day, just as she had. It seemed an eternity ago she'd stood at the bus stop; and she might not even be here now if it hadn't been for Tristan. She pictured him waiting outside for her already, and for some reason that comforted her, despite her earlier impatience with him.

"Are you gonna smile, or what?" the man said. Marlena straightened and put on her best smile. "That's good," he said as the camera's shutter clicked in rapid-fire succession. "Now turn around." Her smile faded a little, but did as he said and turned her back to the camera. It clicked some more. "Okay, turn around and take the dress off."

Marlena stiffened. Did she hear him correctly? Take her dress off?

"Hey. Like I said, haven't got all day, Marlene."

His tone of voice made her start to panic; she was annoying him with her hesitance. This was a business, after all; and hadn't she already prepared herself to do whatever was asked from behind a camera? Just do it, her brain whispered. She reached behind her neck for the zipper's tab and pulled it downward. The soft material skidded off her shoulders and fell to her waist.

Marlena's heart pounded as the cool air brushed her exposed skin. With shaking hands, she pushed the dress past her hips and let the dress fall around her ankles. She stepped out of the ring of fabric and stood there, clad only in her plain white bra and panties. Her arms wrapped protectively around herself. Doing a thing was much harder than imagining doing a thing, she realized. Instead of beautiful and confident, she felt as awkward as one of the newborn lambs on her family's farm, and just as scared.

"Arms down," the voice snapped. She dropped her arms to her sides, lowering her eyes to the floor. The voice clucked in disdain. "You want the job or not? Look at the camera, doll."

Marlena's head snapped up. The spotlights glared in her face, the heat radiating from them doing little to stop her shivering. "Yes, I want the job." The camera sputtered multiple shots. Gooseflesh rose all over her body and her nipples hardened, straining against the cups of her bra; only this time it was not pleasurable like before.

"That's a good girl." The voice seemed to soften, and lowered in pitch. "Yeah. Keep that look." More camera clicks. "Don't stand like you've got a pole down your back. Feet apart; put one hand on your hip." Marlena relaxed a bit, feeling more comfortable the more she moved around; feeling like a model. She posed as he directed, striking the same stance facing away from the camera. This wasn't so bad. And after all, how else would they know if she was model material if she didn't show her body? Still, she wished they would finish soon. She wanted to put her clothes back on.

"Okay turn around. Lose the bra."

"What?" The question slipped from her lips before she could stop it.

"Don't pretend you don't understand. Take it off. Show us your tits."

Marlena felt frozen, unable to respond. His words shocked her. So crude and vulgar. How dare he speak to her like that. "No," she finally said, shaking her head. "I can't."

"Don't waste my time, little girl. We're done here." Panic rose again. She'd blown it; the very thing she didn't want to do. It felt so wrong, what he asked; but she couldn't afford to say no. Not now. Not when she'd gone this far.

"I'm not a little girl," she said, her voice barely above a squeak.

"Prove it. Show me your tits, or get out."

Chapter Sixteen

Ernesto pushed through the doorway of the Sanchez villa, practically knocking Consuelo over before she could step back. "Is Marly here?" he asked, his voice breathless and strained. His mind replayed the moments he'd last seen Marlena, the harsh words he'd spoken. He didn't mean them, and regretted all of them.

He'd waited for her after school, to apologize and set things right again. Even if it meant parting ways, he couldn't live with this rift between them, and would do anything to repair it. When the school bus had departed and still no sign of Marly, he searched the nearly-empty school hallways and classrooms for her. She had simply vanished. He trudged the miserable distance home, and though he wasn't to take it without permission, immediately jumped into his father's work truck and drove to the villa, feverishly hoping she'd gotten there some other way.

"No, Senor Allesandro. She not here," Consuelo answered brusquely, clearly indicating her indignation with his unseemly entrance. "You were not expected. What is it you want?"

Ernesto exhaled in exasperation, running one hand through his unruly hair and adjusting his glasses that had slid down the sweaty bridge of his nose with the other. "I must see her mother. Is she at home?"

After a stiff appraisal of his appearance, Consuelo gave a curt nod. "I tell Senora Bianca you here."

Ernesto paced the brick and stone foyer until Bianca appeared. "Ernesto. A surprise to see you," the lady of the house began, pausing as she took in his demeanour. "Whatever is wrong? You seem upset."

"I can't find Marly. She wasn't on the bus home, and I'm worried. Do you know where she is?"

"I believe she wanted to do a little shopping after school," Bianca said. "She had some money saved up and asked if she could buy some new clothes. We hope to hear from the modeling school any day now." Bianca smiled and leaned toward him a bit. "She wants to be a model, you know."

Suddenly, the tension in Ernesto's body released, leaving him feeling boneless and a little embarrassed. Of course, there was a logical explanation; he'd jumped to conclusions again, like he'd been doing a lot lately. Ever since that British gringo had arrived, it seemed. But he found it hard to be logical where Marlena was concerned. His feelings for her had always been strong, and they were increasing day by day; changing, growing desperate. He nodded his head and gazed down at the floor. "Yes, I…she told me. But she never said anything about going shopping today."

Bianca chuckled and placed a hand on his shoulder. "Well, women can't tell their men everything, you know. We always need a little mystery to keep the good ones around." Ernesto raised his head, her words lighting a tiny flame of hope. "Do you want to wait here for her?" she asked.

As much as he wanted to do just that, Ernesto didn't like the vision of what Marly might think when she saw him waiting around for her like a lost puppy. He was stronger than that, and he had to show it. "Thank you, but no. I've intruded here enough, Senora. I'll call later."

"It's no intrusion," Bianca said, releasing her touch. "I'll tell her you were here."

"No, don't do that. I mean, she probably knows I'd come by," Ernesto said, disguising his anxiety with false bravado. "Sorry to trouble you. Goodbye, Senora Sanchez." He left the house and strode to his truck as though iron was in his spine. If Marly didn't tell him her plans, there was a reason. Clearly, she didn't want him hanging around; or at least hanging around while she picked out dresses and shoes. That, he could understand. But her attitude had been more hostile than that.

He rolled the other parts of their conversation around in his head. "I'm going to Madrid," she'd said. That wasn't news; they'd even talked about going there together. Recalling that fact sent a stab of remorse through him. She'd given him that chance, and he ignored it. Now she'd be going without him. Alone.

Or maybe not alone.

Could she have meant that literally? Going to Madrid… today? He started the engine and put the gear in reverse, backing down the long driveway at full throttle, ignoring the bone-shaking bumps. If she wasn't alone, he had a good idea who might be with her. He had to know.

In minutes, Ernesto braked to a hard stop in front of the Gracia Immaculata. He raced up the steps and burst through the main doors into the sanctuary. The Pastor would be in his office or the rectory, and against his upbringing, ran full speed up the center aisle and toward the back rooms of the church. "Pastor Giorgio," he called ahead.

His head swiveled as he entered the rectory, looking for the man. The Pastor stood in the doorway of his small office, responding to all the ruckus. "Ernesto," Don Giorgio said, a look of concern on his face. "What brings you here, and in such a rush?"

"Is Tristan here?" he asked point-blank.

The Pastor shook his head. "He is not. And I'm becoming concerned. I hope there wasn't an accident."

"An accident?" Ernesto said, blinking through lenses that were fogging from his heavy breathing. "What do you mean?"

Don Giorgio stepped closer toward him, spreading his hands wide. "He went to work in town today, doing some excavating for a project with the town counsel. He wasn't sure how long it would take, or even be successful, but hasn't yet returned. Digging is hard, risky work. I hope he hasn't been injured."

"He's been gone all day?" To Ernesto, that meant two possibilities. He had either been occupied, and therefore not with Marlena; or, used the project as an excuse to be away for the entire day with her. "Where in town?"

"Somewhere near El Guardián. I believe it was to do with an irrigation plan. He took young Ángel with him as a helper. Why are you looking for him?"

Ernesto hadn't thought as far as having to explain his reasons. He'd hoped to find Tristan at the church and confront him directly, but now the question hung in the air. "Senora Sanchez asked me to find him. I was coming to town anyway, and…there's a…mechanical problem she thought he could help with." He cringed at having to lie to a clergyman, but decided to keep going with it. "Who is Ángel?"

"A little boy from town. Ángel Ibanez. He lives with his mother on Calle Verdugo. I'm afraid he's rather taken with our Senor Flynn; been spending a lot of time with him. Misses his father, I expect." Don Giorgio folded his arms as he cast his kindly gaze over Ernesto. "Why don't you sit down. You seem out of breath, my son. What troubles you? Do you wish to talk about it?"

Ernesto sank onto one of the benches at the rectory table. He didn't want to talk about it, exactly; but he was running out of ideas. If he could talk to anyone, surely a church Pastor would be a good choice. "I'm sorry, Padre. I wasn't entirely honest with you. I've come for a different reason." He took a deep breath. "Marlena is missing. We thought…that is, I thought… Tristan might have…they might have run off together."

The Pastor looked taken aback; his brows rising in surprise. Then he shook his balding head. "I think you're mistaken. Why would you say such a thing?"

"Because he wants her," Ernesto blurted out. "Don't you see that? He has from the beginning."

Don Giorgio uncrossed his arms and brought his palms together in a calming gesture. "I cannot confirm or deny any such thing. Be that as it may, you say Senorita Sanchez is missing? That is serious. How long has she been gone? Oh dear, her poor mother must be distraught."

Ernesto flinched inwardly, realizing that the only person feeling distraught was himself. Marly's mother wasn't the least bit worried; and he had only his own jealous suspicions to go on. "When Marlena wasn't on the school bus home I got worried and went to her house. Her mother thought she had gone shopping after school, but had not yet come home."

"Well, then, perhaps that's all there is to it."

"You don't know Marly like I do; and you don't know what's been going on between her and…and him. I just feel something bad has happened."

"Why don't we go and see?" Don Giorgio suggested. "Let's walk into town and have a look in the shops. If she's there, that will set your mind at ease, yes?"

Ernesto nodded in resignation. If nothing else, he could talk to her. She wouldn't brush him off with the good Pastor in tow.

"And I may also find out what has become of my miracle worker," Don Giorgio continued, reaching for his cloak. "Shall we go then, Senor Alvarez?"

Chapter Seventeen

Tears of humiliation welled in Marlena's eyes as she reached for the closure on her bra and unhooked it. She dropped the white lace thing to the floor, her nude breasts in full view and nipples standing to attention. The camera clicked rapidly.

"Good girl. You want to be in movies, don't you?" The voice was smooth now, low and quiet. "Speak up, so I can hear your voice."

Movies? The ad never said anything about movies. "What do you want me to say," Marlena asked, staring blankly ahead, forcing back tears.

"Say how you like to be touched."

She wasn't sure what he meant. "Touched?"

"Yeah. How your boyfriend likes to touch you."

Of all the questions she could be asked, that wasn't one of them. It occurred to her they never asked her name; she'd provided it willingly. They didn't ask her to fill out any forms or if she had any experience, and now they were talking about movies. Had she made a mistake…a terrible mistake? A dark wave of remorse began to engulf her. She was trapped in this awful place, naked and vulnerable and above all, ashamed. She wished she'd never seen that newspaper.

"Well? Cat got your tongue?" he demanded.

"I don't have a boyfriend."

The voice went silent for an agonizing minute. Her face blushed hot with embarrassment. Dios, she wanted to crawl away and hide. "A pretty girl like you? Don't lie. Touch your breasts and imagine its him touching you."

Marlena squeezed her eyes shut, as though seeing nothing would make everything not real; make everything she'd done and would do next be like it never happened. Afraid to hear what the voice might say next, she raised her hands to her chest. She remembered standing at the bullring with Tristan's arms around her, and how her breasts had tingled to life against his strong body. Her fingers brushed the hardened nubs of her nipples, and it made them tighten even further. Her panties felt wet, just like that day in her bedroom. No, not here. Please not here.

"That's good. More. Squeeze those tits. Tell me how it feels." The tears she'd been holding back spilled down her cheeks as she cupped her breasts, hiding her throbbing nipples. "Does it feel good?" the voice prodded. She shook her head. "Mierda! Don't cry. Only little girls cry. Little girls don't star in movies. You're still just a little girl, aren't you?"

"No," she sobbed.

"I don't believe you. Just a little girl from the country, right?"

"I'm a grown woman," she cried, her blubbering only serving to prove she was not. She felt frightened and miserable. She sniffled a wet breath, sounding more like a child than ever.

The man fell silent again while she stood there trembling. "Take off your panties and prove it," he finally said.

*

Tristan kept his eyes on the dark glass door, but saw nothing. It had been close to an hour since Marlena had passed through it, and he was getting angry. The yellowed newspaper clipping had been so mangled, he could barely make out the print. His knowledge of Spanish was improving, but not enough to understand all the half-obliterated words. From the few that he recognized, the ad did appear legitimately seeking applicants. Modelos, he presumed meant models, since Marlena had talked about going to modeling school.

But what kind of modeling? Clothes? Jewelry? Posing for painters or sculptors? The latter made him even more uneasy; he remembered the art students at university sketching nude models in the studios. He hoped it was fashion modeling, but even that made him think of lingerie ads in clothing catalogues. He shifted uncomfortably in his seat, keeping an anxious eye on the blackened glass door for another long minute. Frustrated, he decided to get out of the vehicle altogether.

Dark had nearly fallen, making the heat even more claustrophobic than it was in broad daylight. He looked up and down the deserted street. Odd that no pedestrians were about, and virtually no other cars had driven down this way. He'd seen bad neighborhoods before, and as the shadows deepened, knew this was one of them. He walked around to the curb side and leaned on the passenger door of the van. His stomach churned with foreboding, the emptiness of the street further heightening his suspicions. Even thugs and pickpockets didn't seem to frequent the area.

Tristan was okay in a fight; thoughts of he and Ari in that backstreet cantina ran through his mind. Ironically, the incident had been nearly two years ago, and the place might only be a mile or two from where he stood now. He'd know what to do if a lone attacker tried to jump him, but what if a whole gang of them suddenly showed up? He had no weapons on him. He thought of his tools in the back of the van, and stepped around to open the rear doors. Two shovels. A steel tape measure. A plumb bob and line. He smiled as his eyes fell on a pipe wrench. He hoisted the heavy tool to his belt.

As he closed the van, he caught a flash of something moving behind the entrance door of the building. He leaped across the sidewalk and grasped the handle, startling the figure on the other side as he wrenched it open. "Mierda," it cussed, stepping back. "Who the fuck are you, we're closed."

"Not yet," Tristan said, shouldering his way in. "A girl came in here. Where is she?"

The lights were off, but he could make out the man's dark bulk in front of him; a stocky body, shorter than himself. The smell of stale cigarette smoke radiated from him. "There's nobody here," he grunted. "Get out, I'm closing up. You're trespassing."

"You can call the cops after I find my friend. Where is she? What kind of place is this?"

"I don't know your friend," the man's gruff voice said. "This is my place of business, and my business is none of yours, amigo. Get lost."

Tristan stepped closer to the man, his grip tightening on the wrench's handle. "She came in here an hour ago. I'm sure you couldn't miss her; pretty, long brown hair."

The man laughed, an ugly, guttural sound, and mirrored Tristan's advance. No more than a few inches stood between them. "Lots of pretty girls in Madrid, amigo," he said, his tone low and suggestive. "Why don't you go find one at Senora Roja's place on the next block…she'll show you a good time."

New voices sounded from somewhere deeper inside the dark space. A man's harsh voice, then a woman's…a woman crying. Instinctively, Tristan swung the wrench at his opponent's head, catching him on the side of his skull with a sickening crack. He pushed past the man's falling body and moved toward the voices. His eyes had adjusted to the light enough to sidestep the few obstacles in the room and head down a tunnel-like hallway. A sliver of light shone through a slightly parted curtain straight ahead.

He broke into a near-run as the woman's cries echoed louder from behind the curtain and ripped it aside as he reached it. He blinked at the sudden glare of light from the center of the room, and then his guts went cold. With spotlights trained on her, Marlena stood in the harsh cone of light, almost completely naked. Her body trembled as she sobbed uncontrollably, vainly trying to cover herself with crossed arms. A dark figure stood just outside the circle of light, his features vaguely outlined by the glare. As Tristan burst into the room, the man's eyeglass lenses flashed a reflection as he turned toward him.

"Get away from her, you perverted fuck," Tristan shouted in a feral growl.

"Nico!" the man screamed, obviously calling for his associate out front.

Tristan rushed forward. "He can't help you," he snarled. "I said get away from her!"

The man backed up, crashing into the lighting stands and knocking them over. "Fuck!" he cursed as he stumbled, briefly revealing his face in the bobbing light, but turned away as he scrambled to his feet and ran from the room.

Marlena had backed away from the skirmish and into the shadows, her sobbing turned to anguished wails. Tristan stepped over a camera and tripod that had also collapsed into the heap of upturned equipment. "Are you alright?" he said, his heart pounding and his breath ragged as he went to her.

She sat huddled in a fetal position, hiding her face. "No! Get away," she cried between sobs. "Don't touch me. Don't look at me." Tristan averted his gaze, and saw her clothes in a heap near were she'd been standing. He reached for them and brought them over.

"I won't look. Here. Are you alright? Did they hurt you?" He crouched a few feet away, his eyes lowered. He realized he still held the heavy wrench in his hand, and wondered if 'Nicc' was still out cold, or worse. Had he killed the brute? He didn't want to find out. They had to get out of here, fast. He shoved the wrench handle inside his belt. The photographer had fled backstage; hopefully there was another exit besides the way he'd come in.

"No," she blubbered, sniffing up her tears. "They said something about being in movies. I thought it was a modeling school, and it would just be photographs…"

Modeling. Tristan thought back to the shred of newspaper Marlena had dropped. It was all a scam. Offering modeling classes, then luring innocent, naive young girls into makeshift porn studios on that pretense. It made his blood boil; God only knew what they did after they took the pictures. Drug them, maybe…hold them captive; make them unrecognizable to anyone who might be looking for them. He'd heard his former workmates talk about pornographic films that were beginning to flood the theaters now that Franco's iron fist was weakening its hold on the populace; and the seeds of evil were sprouting from between his failing fingers.

"Shhh," he quieted. "It's okay. It's over now." While Marlena dressed, he quickly picked up the fallen camera then returned to help her to her feet. "We have to get out of here, fast."

Chapter Eighteen

Marlena choked back a sob and allowed Tristan to lift her from the floor. Her fingernails dug into his strong forearms as he did so, not only to hold on, but to stop her limbs from shaking. No time to think now, about fear or shame or embarrassment; the need to escape from this place was all that mattered. As he led her in the direction the photographer had gone, Marlena clasped Tristan's hand like a lifeline, shutting out everything from her mind except the warmth of his grip, blindly trusting he would get them both to safety.

What if the photographer jumped them in the darkness? And what about the man in the front office? Surely he'd heard all the commotion. Whoever they were, those two men knew the building, and neither she or Tristan did. She prayed there was a back door of some kind and they would find it quickly without running into either of them. Suddenly, Tristan changed direction and nearly jerked her arm out of its socket. "There," he whispered.

Wincing against the pain, Marlena saw a dim square of light ahead, and was pulled toward it. As they got nearer, the shape became recognizable as a grimy window set into a heavy door. Tristan threw his weight against it and the pair of them stumbled out into a darkened alley. Humid air carried the fetid smells of garbage and human waste to their nostrils, but she didn't care. It was the smell of freedom.

"Come on," he said, ushering her away from the building and down the narrow alley. They emerged on the main street, and she saw their rusted blue van parked several yards away. The area was deserted, with no sign of either man from inside the building. Panting for breath, Marlena's knees buckled and felt herself slipping to the ground. Strong arms went around her waist and held her to stand again. "We have to keep going," Tristan whispered, his voice hoarse with urgency. "Just a little farther."

He half-dragged her to the van and quickly deposited her inside, tossing the wrench and the camera in the back. In a flash he was behind the wheel, the vehicle lurching away from the curb and speeding down the street. Marlena huddled in the passenger seat and turned her face toward the window. The emotions she kept at bay while escaping now filled her all at once; shame, embarrassment, relief, remorse. She couldn't face Tristan like this.

She'd been estupid. Stupid enough to believe a vague ad in a newspaper, stupid enough to believe everything she read. Even the torn magazine she kept under her mattress she'd accepted as truth. In addition to feeling duped, Marlena suddenly felt small, a tiny, insignificant thing that knew nothing at all about the world. How did she expect to succeed, to rise above her life that she considered so mundane, to want more than what she had? Perhaps there was nothing more for girls like her; become someone's wife and have no ambitions except to cook, clean and have babies. She was foolish to think otherwise. But she felt dirty, now. Soiled. Ruined from even having that kind of a future.

"Are you sure you're alright?" Tristan asked, breaking the silence that filled the cab of the van.

Marlena curled her body up even tighter. "Yes." She was physically alright, but her pride had been wounded beyond repair. She could barely speak. What did he think of her now? All the feelings he'd stirred within her with his kiss, with the closeness of his body…whatever had begun to grow between them seemed lost, just as any chance of living the life she'd dreamed of.

"Here." Tristan offered her one of the sodas, the glass bottle sweaty and dripping with condensation. "I'm sorry," he said after an uncomfortable silence. "Sorry that I didn't go in there with you. I should have gone with you."

Marlena had only her own naivete to blame. If he hadn't come in when he did, she might still be there, at the mercy of those horrible men. She took the bottle with shaking hands, and raised it to her lips. She should be grateful; he'd rescued her, yet he was apologizing. She felt worse than shamed; she felt shameful for not even thanking him, but the words would not come. She took a sip of soda to ease her throat. "I told you not to," she finally said, the statement coming out more harshly than she intended.

"I did as you asked, against my better judgment," he said. He slapped the wheel angrily. "Flaming hell, why didn't I stop you. I had a feeling that place meant trouble." She could feel him turn his gaze on her, hot and accusing. "What did they say to you? Did they threaten you? Make you do whatever they said? Or do you just take your clothes off for anyone who asks?"

Marlena's cheeks burned, with more than embarrassment. Anger flared inside her at his words. "I do not," she spat. "I was being professional. It's what models do."

"That was not modeling. Did you not see what was wrong with what they were asking you to do? They took advantage of you."

"I don't want to talk about it," she cried, tears returning to her eyes.

"I think that was a porn ring," Tristan continued. "Do you realize what could have happened? They could have drugged you, beaten you. Made it so that you didn't even remember your name or where you came from. Then filmed you being… doing…" He broke off, leaving the sentence unfinished. "You'd have disappeared, never saw your family again." She looked away again, her misery deepening. "Or me," he added. "And I don't think I could bear that."

She let his words sink in as she watched the streets of Madrid slip past through her tear-blurred eyes. He hated what she'd done, but he didn't hate her, even after she'd made the biggest mistake of her life. That's what friends did. But is that all he wanted? To be her friend? At that moment she realized she wanted more than his friendship; that a bigger mistake would be to turn away from this man. Her inner voice spoke clearer, louder; validating what she felt deep down. They'd met for a reason, their fates inextricably bound together.

"Let's get you home," Tristan said, interrupting her thoughts. "Your mother must be beside herself with worry by now."

Marlena bowed her head. Go home? The idea made her heart pound and her stomach twist. What would she say? What would her mama say? How could she explain any of this? Her mother had never punished her for anything before, but she'd never given her reason before. Her grandmother had beaten Aunt Juliana without a second thought; perhaps Bianca was capable of doing the same. Her limbs began to tremble.

"No! I can't go home. Not now, not yet," she said. "Please don't."

Tristan looked at her. "You have to go home. Where else can you go?"

"I can go with you. Please. If you want to go back to the church, I'll go with you; just don't take me home. I can't face them."

Tristan sighed but kept driving. "It's three hours or more, at night," he said. "We're tired. I think I know a place we can stay, get something to eat, if I can find it. It's been awhile since I've been there."

"Where?"

"A small place. Near the edge of town. The rooms are cheap, and…"

"It sounds fine. I have money." Even as she said it, she realized her bag had been left behind. Her ID and her money. She couldn't even offer to help pay for lodging, or food. Her stomach rumbled. Nether of them had eaten since they left Zaragoza.

Tristan shook his head. "Don't worry about that. You just need to rest, and so do I."

They drove on in silence, the city thinning as they moved farther from its center. The paved streets turned to cobble, and then to dirt. Not even streetlights seemed to exist this far out. Marlena looked upward, seeing with wondrous clarity the stars of the infinite cosmos overhead, and felt very small, indeed.

Tristan slowed as he made one last corner and pulled to a stop alongside a low roofed adobe building, with rounded windows carved out of the walls and its clay-tiled roof missing several tiles. Strings of bare light bulbs hung just under the roof line, the only illumination on the exterior. A small neon sign flashed in one of the porthole-shaped windows, alternately displaying the words 'Cantina' and 'Open'.

"Doesn't look like it's changed much," Tristan said, shifting into park and killing the engine.

"How do you know this place?" Marlena asked, glancing warily at the run-down exterior. Nothing about it was welcoming. But it did seem an appropriate place for hiding out, jammed in among other similarly questionable establishments and backing on to a narrow alley.

"I stopped here once before; shortly after I arrived in Spain." He paused. "It's where I first saw your Aunt Juliana." Marlena looked at him in surprise. This is where it happened, all the things her tía had told her about. They were true! "Come on, let's go inside."

"I can wait here," she said, uncertain why she felt so hesitant. She'd been in a far worse situation just hours ago. Perhaps it was a feeling of foreboding, of mal suerte, since hearing her tía's story.

"Not a chance," he replied, shaking his head. "I'm never letting you out of my sight again." Marlena shivered, even as the hot, humid night air settled on her skin. Walking inside a place with such bad history was far more desirable than the humiliation of returning home, or being left alone. She never wanted to be left alone again. Tristan hurried to her side of the van and opened the door, his strong hand closing firmly yet gently around her wrist. "I'll take care of you."

She looked into his eyes and saw strength, trust and something more; something meant only for her. The glow from the dim strings of bulbs illuminated his curly blond hair like a halo around his head. Angels wore halos. With sudden clarity, she realized she'd met her own guardian angel. She clasped his muscled bicep with her other hand and willingly slipped from her seat to stand firmly on the ground next to him. "I know," she said.

Chapter Nineteen

The bed was small and sagged a bit in the middle. A patchwork quilt, clearly handmade with its random squares of mismatched fabric, draped over it. Only a single chair, a rickety bedside table and the lamp sitting atop it comprised the remaining furniture in the room. "It's not much," Tristan said. "But it's private."

A wisp of night breeze slipped through the open porthole window and caressed Marlena's forehead. Her apprehension had dissipated the moment Tristan helped her across the threshold of the room. Something about it, about being with him, made her feel safe and relaxed. It felt like a sanctuary. The traditional crucifix hung above the head of the bed seemed to validate the thought. For all her railing against tradition, this simple wooden icon suddenly brought her peace, and tears to her eyes. She'd made so many mistakes this day; so many wrong turns and unfortunate consequences. Yet redemption was always just a prayer away.

"Hey," Tristan said, his voice quiet and compassionate. His arms went around her and drew her close. She rested her head against his solid chest. "I'm sorry about the room. I know it's pathetic. I'd take you to a five-star hotel if I could."

His words reminded her of all Tía Juliana had said. "Like the one you used to run? On the coast?" she murmured into his shirt.

"How did you know about that?" he asked.

"Tía Juliana told me everything. Well, nearly everything. That she used to be a dancer here, and that two men fought over her and you stopped them. Then she came to your hotel looking for work."

"El Mirador," Tristan said, his whispered words seeming full of regret. "Yes, she came there."

Silence hung between them for a moment. Marlena could hear the steady, comforting beat of his heart inside his chest and smell his scent. An earthy, fresh fragrance like leaves on a forest floor after a rain, overlaid with the smell of soap and unlaundered clothing. Again, a fluttering sensation gripped her stomach, and a tingling ache began at the tips of her breasts.

Her arms went around his waist and she pressed herself harder against him, fitting her womanly curves into the hard planes and hollows of Tristan's fit body. They were alone, with no one to object or judge them. No one to say what should or should not happen between them. Not even God. She'd felt shame at being naked before those awful men, but knew she would not feel that way here, with him.

She lifted her head and brought her lips close to his. A stubbled growth of beard scraped her chin. "I don't need a five-star hotel," she said, her voice soft and breathless. "I need to grow up. I'm tired of being treated like a child. Can you show me? Show me how to be a woman?"

"If you're asking what I think you're asking," he said, his lips brushing hers, his arms pulling her even deeper into his embrace. "I'm not sure I can. Not like this, not after what you went through today. God, if you'd only asked me a week ago, a month ago…"

"A month ago, I was a disobedient, naïve little brat who didn't listen to anyone but her own stubborn, ridiculous ideas. I don't want to be her anymore."

"You can't blame yourself for what happened," Tristan sighed, his lips trailing soft kisses across her cheek, under her ear and against the spot on her throat where her hot blood pulsed in rapid tempo. She could hear his breath coming heavier, faster, heating her skin with each tight exhale. "What did they do to you," he murmured between kisses, the hardness below his belt growing and pressing into her belly, "…to make you say such things?"

Marlena felt an uncontrollable spasm ripple through her abdomen and settle between her legs, releasing a delicious slickness over her tender privates. She wanted his touch there, between her moist folds, to bring again that dark, overwhelming and indescribable sensation of joy rushing over her, the need achingly sharp. "They made me see what a foolish, silly girl I was. They told me to go home. I wouldn't listen. I begged to stay. I trusted them, total strangers," she sobbed. "More than I trusted you, or anyone who cared about me."

Tristan cradled the back of her head with one hand and framed her cheek with the other, locking their faces close to each other. "I care about you, Marlena Sanchez," he said, his voice raw and crackling with emotion. "If you don't care for me, or don't trust me, then I'd better take you home right now. Because I don't think I can hold you like this another second without making love to you…"

His words were lost as she moved first, claiming his lips in a searing kiss that left no question of her trust unanswered. He responded with equal heat, matching the passion that poured forth from her, their tongues seeking and exploring, the flames of desire fueled by an energy drawn from the very depths of their souls.

"Say you want this," Tristan whispered, breaking their burning kiss, his hands finding the zipper tab of her dress and pulling downward. "Say you want me, Marlena."

"I want you," she gasped, her fingers diving into his mass of curling blond locks. "I want you to take me away, and to be with you, always," Her lips found his again, emphasizing her words and trapping his groan in his throat with her fervent kiss. He untangled her fingertips from his tousled mane and lowered her arms to slip the dress down over her shoulders. His palms caressed the nude skin of her arms as he slid the garment downward, dropping it to the floor as she lifted her hands out and away, only to have them fly to the buttons of his shirt and begin to work them free.

As the last button gave way, their bodies separated of one accord, pausing to drink in the sight of one another. Marlena pushed the material of his shirt aside, her hands exploring the smooth, muscled contours of his chest, breathing out a sigh of wonder. Months of physical work had sculpted his body into hard perfection, from his rounded pectorals to the washboard ripples of his midsection. He closed his eyes for a moment, his head tilting back slightly as her touch flowed over him before he reached for his belt and began pulling the buckle free. She watched in fascination as he popped the rivet on the waistband and split the zipper of his jeans open, releasing the stiffened mass that had pressed so urgently against her.

She wanted to touch it but before she could, Tristan opened his eyes, his blue gaze deepening to an intense, ultramarine hue that seemed to penetrate the very core of her being. He cupped her breasts with both hands, exploring their firm texture with gentle but urgent fingers. Her nipples swelled to aching hardness beneath her bra, and the place between her legs vibrated wildly with need. "You're so beautiful, Marlena…you have no idea what the sight of you does to me."

His words only added to the desire she felt bursting within, and arched into his touch as she reached behind and released the closure of her brassiere, allowing the cups to spring free in his hands. He whisked the skimpy garment away and took full possession of her naked breasts in his palms, rubbing the diamond-hard tips of her nipples with his thumbs. "Dios mio," he whispered, as he bent his head to take one hardened brown disk into his mouth. She felt the warmth of his tongue as it circled her aching nipple, and gasped in sweet pain as he sucked it deep into his eager mouth.

Her body ignited with the multiple sensations of his hands and lips on her breasts, his wiry blond hair and rough beard brushing her heated skin. Her panties were soaked with a renewed gush of her excited juices. She whimpered in helpless submission. "Tristan…"

As she said his name, he released her breast. She shivered visibly as cool air met wet flesh, the round orb of her breast glistening in the muted light of the tiny room. "Trust me," he murmured into her ear. Then he bent and lifted her slight body off the floor, moving them both toward the sad but available bed. He laid her down on it, her dark tresses fanning out over the single pillow. She lay still, looking up at him as he stood above her, his eyes shining with undisguised desire.

"Let me see you," she whispered. "All of you, as you see me…as God made us. Show me what a man truly and fully looks like."

His lips curled in a wry grin, and shrugged his opened shirt off his shoulders and onto the floor. Marlena tilted her head as it rested on the feather-stuffed pillow, admiring what she saw, the soft light reflecting off every line and curve of his upper body, from broad shoulders to bulging biceps. When he shoved his well-worn jeans downward, she marveled at the flex of muscled thighs and the sinewy working of tendons. Her questions of the male physique were now answered in full, and she drew in a breath as his aroused cock was revealed; rigid, swollen and rippled with veins.

Tossing the denims aside, Tristan stood still before her in all his naked male glory, allowing her a moment to observe as she wished, and satisfy her curiosity. Her eyes took all of him in, and her tongue darted out to moisten her lips in anticipation of what was to come next. All the mystique and secrecy she'd been indoctrinated with her whole life about men and women, about sex and marriage and decency and the sanctity of her virginity felt like so much rubbish now. There was nothing to fear or be ashamed of here. She wanted this man and he wanted her. Nothing could be simpler or more beautiful.

"Do you like what you see?" he asked playfully, echoing the words she'd spoken to him in the kitchen in what seemed so long ago.

Marlena nodded silently, and reached out for him, beckoning him nearer. He strode to the side of the bed, where she took his stiff cock in her hands, stroking its tight skin and hardened ridges, exploring every inch of its surface. Tristan groaned and stilled her hands. "Wait."

"I'm sorry, does that hurt you?" she asked, worried that perhaps she'd done the wrong thing. The stretched and reddened skin looked painful to her.

"No," he chuckled, shaking his curly head. "Far from it. But you're going to kill me if you keep doing it," he said. "I'd die a happy man, but if I'm to die of happiness, I want it to be inside you, making love to you." He removed her hands from his body and lowered himself to the bed, lying partly on top of her. A thrill rushed through her, starting between her legs and rocketing up her spine. He kissed her again, his tongue thrusting deep inside the wet, warm cave of her mouth. Her pussy began to ache.

Tristan worked his kisses downward, from her lips to her throat to her breasts, licking and sucking each one in turn until she thought she would explode with desire. As his tongue swirled and flicked each rock-hard nipple, his hand stroked her belly, moving downward in soft circles until he reached her panties. She gasped out loud as he placed his hand between her legs and palmed her sex, the wet fabric pressing against her pussy as he rubbed and squeezed.

"It's alright," he whispered. "Let yourself go, I've got you; I'll take care of you."

Marlena's heart thudded in her ears and her breath came short; she could hear herself panting, wild with lust. Tristan slipped his hand beneath the waistband of her soaked panties and tugged them down as he kissed a path down her belly and abdomen. She lifted her hips on instinct, allowing him to slip the last barrier between them out from under her and down the length of her legs.

At last they were both naked, skin to skin. It felt wonderful and natural; how could this ever be thought of as sinful? Everything she'd been taught about sex was completely untrue. It was breathtakingly beautiful. Tristan rested his head on her belly as his hand traveled back between her legs, stroking the sensitive skin of her inner thighs, urging them apart. She spread her legs, wanting nothing more than to open to him completely. She was his, body and soul.

His fingers plied her wet folds, teasing the sensitive bud near the top of her labia. Marlena's whole body jerked as he worked it in tiny circles, then up and down, side to side. The mysterious, powerful rush of sensation she craved more of began to build with each move of his fingertip. "Dios," she moaned.

"You're so beautiful, Marlena," he murmured. "I want this to be so good for you. You feel so good, let yourself feel good. Don't fight it." He slipped his finger inside her soft entrance as he spoke his sweet words. Her eyes went wide, and her private muscles clenched around his finger as he moved it gently in and out. When he pulled it free and touched her bud again, the beautiful wave she'd felt from afar rushed forward and overtook her in a storm of ecstasy.

"Tristan!" she cried aloud. Her mind blanked, every thought drowned in the deluge except for him, his name; knowing that he was with her, ushering her lovingly through this forbidden heaven.

"That's a girl, let it come, baby," he urged, maintaining his erotic touch, nurturing her throbbing bud forward through orgasm. As the waves began to recede, her tender privates still convulsing, he drew his body overtop her once more.

He raised one of her legs so that her foot rested in the small of his back, the tip of his engorged cock poised at her virgin entrance. She sucked in a breath and dug her nails into his muscled arms. "I love you, Marly," he whispered, his handsome face level with hers, his clear blue eyes full of tenderness and truth.

She'd never heard those words spoken to her; never heard the name Marly sound so right as it did coming from the lips of this man. She surrendered to him completely, and felt a gentle pressure as he breached her outer lips. His fully primed cock pushed deeper, stretched her untried walls when suddenly, a searing sting raked through her lower body. She let out a strangled cry at the sharp yet sweet pain.

She was his, now and forever.

Chapter Twenty

Ernesto awoke to the sounds of birds chirping in the murky dawn. For a moment he felt disoriented, his surroundings unfamiliar, but soon recognized the features of Villa Sanchez. He raised his upper body from the wooden bench on which he'd slept, paying no mind to the stiffness in his back because of it. He rubbed his eyes and peered all around, seeing nothing in the quiet dimness, but felt certain he was not the only one awake. Senora Sanchez had likely been up all night.

He'd returned to Marlena's home when his search of downtown with Pastor Giorgio turned up fruitless. They saw no sign of her on any of the shopping streets and no-one they spoke with had remembered seeing her. Unless she'd somehow snuck into the villa while he was asleep, she was still missing, and his heart felt as though twisted and squeezed into a bloody pulp with worry. He'd asked permission to stay and stand vigil near the front doors. Though there were other ways to gain entry to the house, it was unlikely she had returned without him knowing.

He sat up fully and gazed out the window. Even the dogs were still asleep. No other vehicles besides his own sat parked outside. He could not even imagine Marlena staying away from home overnight, or how she could have lied, even to her mother, about her true plans. Worse thoughts began to grip him; what if she'd been abducted? By someone else entirely? Tristan's disappearance might have been coincidence. But Ernesto didn't think so. He and Marly were together somewhere, he was sure of it.

Ernesto wandered into the kitchen and sat down. A bowl of fruit was laid out in the center and he helped himself to an orange to ease his growling stomach. He wanted to search the house to be certain she hadn't come home during the night, but it was not his place to do so. As he bit into a juicy section of orange, he heard footsteps on the stairs. He turned to see a pale, anxious version of the normally vibrant, elegant Bianca enter the kitchen. Her eyes seemed hollowed from lack of sleep and her body language spoke of nervous exhaustion.

"Ernesto," she said, managing a small smile. "Did you really stay the whole night?"

"Si, Senora. I didn't see or hear anything, but I did fall asleep. Have you heard anything?"

Bianca shook her head. "She's nowhere in the house. Her bed hasn't been slept in. Everything in her room is just as she left it." She joined him at the table and exhaled in a defeated sigh. "Where could she be, Ernesto?" How could she lie to me?"

He swallowed his piece of orange with difficulty, thinking of how he could voice his suspicions to her. "Perhaps she didn't," he said quietly.

"What do you mean?"

He shook his head. "I don't want to worry you even more but, it's possible she was abducted."

Bianca's tired eyes widened. "You mean kidnapped? By whom? Why? For money?"

"Not for money. For something more precious."

Bianca straightened in her chair. "What are you saying, Ernesto," she said, her voice low and quavering. "If you know something you must tell me."

Ernesto took a deep breath. "I think Tristan Flynn planned this. He wants her, Senora; I'm sure you know that. I think he took her and went to Madrid."

"That cannot be," Bianca gasped. "Senor Flynn is an honorable young man. If he was interested in my daughter, he would have asked my permission to call on her, and Pastor Giorgio would certainly know his whereabouts. And Madrid? That's a long way away from here, why would they go there? Why would you say such a thing?"

"Honor!" Ernesto scoffed. "That's what he wants, Senora… to take her honor, her innocence!" He could not bring himself to say it more plainly. "I'm sorry but with respect, you don't know what's been going on. I've seen them together. They were holding each other and kissing," he said, spitting out his last word like an olive pit. "He's the farthest thing from honorable. He's a wolf among sheep." Bianca looked horrified. Finally, perhaps someone would look at Tristan in the same light that he did. "With your permission, I could go after them," he suggested.

She only stared at him in disbelief. "No. We need to go to the police. Where would you even begin to look? You don't know for certain what's happened," she said.

Ernesto doubted the police would take any action. Marly was eighteen and couldn't be considered a missing person until a day or two had passed, but he could see her mother was distraught. Perhaps she even doubted Ernesto's ability to help, and had more faith in the police than in himself. He wanted to find Marlena more than ever. "Call the police if you want, but I'm going to look for her anyway. Thank you for allowing me to stay the night."

He rose from the table and left the house, feeling angry, hurt and frustrated in addition to worried sick; but Bianca had a point. Where would he even begin to look in a big city like Madrid? He didn't know his way around. He wasn't even sure he could afford the gas it would take to get there, and it would be hours away in any case. But he had to do something.

He went outside where the first rays of sunrise struggled to emerge from behind a cloudy horizon and got into his truck. He drove out of the Sanchez property, not knowing where to go and uncertain of his next step. As he reached to road that led to town, he could think of only one thing. He remembered the Pastor mentioning a young boy that had been helping Tristan. Perhaps he knew something. Clinging to that idea, he headed back toward town and the Gracia Immaculata, hoping Don Giorgio was an early riser.

*

The sky had completely clouded over by the time Ernesto followed the Pastor's directions and arrived at a small dwelling sandwiched between two similar adjoining ones on Calle Verdugo. The overcast conditions made the entire town seem gray and desolate, and a perpetual dry wind caused by the relentless drought whistled through the streets, stirring up dust and debris. His stomach felt as barren as the windswept townscape before him. He'd eaten nothing but that orange since yesterday, but couldn't worry about food right now. He knocked on the sagging wooden door of the house, and was met by a thin boy with dark hair and wide eyes. "Are you Ángel Ibanez?" he asked.

"Si. Do you wish to see my mother?"

"No. Pastor Giorgio sent me to talk to you. Have you seen Senor Tristan Flynn?" The boy looked him up and down, a hint of suspicion on his face. "My name is Ernesto, and I'm a friend of his," he added. The term of friend was a bit of a stretch, but he had to at least introduce himself and gain the boy's trust.

"Si. I saw him yesterday," the boy said. "He lives at the church."

"I know that, but he didn't return there yesterday, and Don Giorgio is very concerned. Do you know where he might have gone?" Ernesto saw a figure come into view behind the boy, and was shocked to see a frail blond woman appear from the shadows, seated in a wheelchair. She moved herself to the boy's side.

"May we help you, senor?" she asked in a quiet, pleasant voice.

"He's looking for El Milagro," Ángel said to her. "No-one has seen him since yesterday."

"Verdad? Is that true? I do hope he hasn't come to any harm. Such a nice man; and he's been so good to us."

"El…Milagro?" Ernesto asked doubtfully. "Why do you call him that?"

"Don't you? He fixed the well; he built this wheelchair," Ángel answered, patting the handlebars of the contraption. "He's saved El Guardián, too. He can make miracles."

Ernesto's blood began to simmer. Nearly everyone he'd spoken to thought of Tristan as some kind of folk hero. Why didn't they see the Welshman for what he really was? An opportunist and a cad. He decided to ignore the boy's last comment. "Well, he's missing. Do you know where he might have gone? Did he say anything to you when you last saw him?"

Ángel thought for a moment. "He said, see you tomorrow."

Ernesto's brow wrinkled. See you tomorrow? That implied Tristan had no intention of leaving. It didn't make sense; but then, what else would he say to a young boy who obviously idolized him? He'd hardly disclose his illicit plans to him.

Ernesto opened his mouth to speak, but closed it quickly as a sudden whirlwind of dust blew across the porch, smattering his face with grains of sand and dirt. "Come inside, por favor," the woman said. Ángel's small hands gripped Ernesto's arm and dragged him forward. He stumbled inside and closed the door behind him, the last gasps of the wind causing curtains to flutter and papers to scatter. He wiped the grit from his face with his sleeve.

"This weather," the woman sighed. "I've never seen such a dry, hot summer." Ernesto rubbed the last of the dust from his eyes and looked in her direction. She gave a warm smile as she backed her wheelchair into the center of the room. Ernesto saw an ancient stove and wooden washstand on one side of the room, and a curtained-off bed in the opposite corner. The single open room appeared to be all the space they had. "Welcome, I'm Carolina Ibanez. You've met my son, Ángel. What is your name?"

"Gracias, senora. I'm Ernesto Alvarez."

"Well, Senior Alvarez, it looks like you may be stuck here for awhile until that wind dies down. Will you have something to eat?"

Despite its meagre appearance, the small abode smelled wonderful; of cinnamon and ginger and newly-baked bread, and Ernest's stomach grumbled once more. He really was hungry, and had run out of ideas on where to find Marlena short of driving to Madrid. His shoulders slumped as he exhaled in resignation. "Si senora," he nodded. "I'd like that very much."

Chapter Twenty-One

"I wish we could stay here forever," Marlena sighed as she lay next to him, her head on his chest and their bodies tangled together in the tiny bed. Morning light beamed in through the porthole window, and the faint sounds of street traffic drifted to Tristan's ears as he wrapped his arms more tightly around her. The only thing he wanted forever was to have this girl in his arms, his heart and his life.

"Surely not here," he murmured into her hair.

He felt her warm body wiggle with laughter. "I meant here with you. Away from everything and everyone."

"Ah, so you're embarrassed to be seen with me, is that it?" he teased. Her hand caressed the taut muscles of his abs. Her touch aroused him instantly, and he felt ready for another round of lovemaking. If his cock had anything to say about it, they could very well be staying here forever.

"Not embarrassed," she said. "Just…"

"Just what?" he prompted, stroking her soft black tresses that were only slightly mussed from their wild, wonderful night. He smiled at the recollection, how she'd melted to his touch, writhed in ecstasy beneath him and cried out his name.

He'd taken the gift of her virginity she'd given freely. He would honor that, and her, for the rest of his life.

She turned her head to look into his face. "You know what will be waiting for us in Zaragoza. My mother, and Ernesto, and the whole villa. Waiting for an explanation; maybe even to punish me."

Her brown eyes, so lovely and full of wide-eyed innocence, gazed into his and seared his soul. Punish her? Did she mean physical punishment? No wonder she didn't want to go back; the idea seemed unthinkable but painfully underscored his position as an outsider. His cultural sensibilities did not apply here.

With a stab of guilt, he realized he was responsible for this, no matter how much she had agreed to their union; no matter that it was her decision to leave without telling anyone. She'd trusted him, and he'd made the situation worse. He'd protected her and saved her from an unimaginable circumstance, but had still failed her in his own way. He wouldn't be seen as her rescuer. He'd be seen as a villain, and she as a victim. "They will be worried, yes, but we've done nothing that you should be punished for." He traced the curve of her cheek with his finger. "We've chosen each other, and they'll have to accept that."

"I want to believe that," she whispered. "But where does that leave us? If we're scorned by my family, by society, we may never be happy here. You can go back to England, but I..."

"Shhh..." he put his finger across her lips. "I will never leave you, Marly. Trust in that. If I return to England, it will be with you by my side. I won't be apart from you, ever."

She kissed his fingers as they brushed across her lips. "How can you be so sure," she said. "You don't know this country; what can happen here. This is not England."

Tristan smiled. "No, it's not. But I assume the law here still allows two people of age to marry each other, does it not?"

Marlena's eyes went wide. "Marry?"

"Matrimonio…that is the word, si? You've heard of it?" he joked; but his intentions were no joke. He would marry this girl, in any country. Nothing would stop him, not family, not politics. "Then we could live in either country, any country; any one you'd like."

She blinked as though clearing her vision of a mirage. "Are you asking me to marry you?"

It wasn't the most romantic proposal, he realized, but he wanted nothing more in the world. "Marlena Sanchez, yes I am. I'd get down on one knee, but there seems to be this beautiful girl lying on top of me. The only girl I want. I hope she'll say yes."

Her brow wrinkled a little, and a smile teased the corners of her mouth. "That's not how it's done here," she said. "You would have to ask permission from my family, and I never said I want to be married. I wanted…"

He pulled her up to his level and kissed her, stopping the words he didn't want to hear from coming out. His lips crushed against hers, and his tongue pressed open the seam of her closed mouth, demanding entry. She surrendered to his sweet invasion, allowing him to explore her wet depths and responding with equal eagerness, her tongue dancing with his and her lips drawing every ounce of passion from his soul.

With difficulty, he broke their kiss, just enough to let her know he understood. "You want a career…as a model, I know. You can have that Marly, I promise you. I'll help you. I would never hold you back, but I will marry you." He dove back into their kiss as though to add an exclamation point. His cock reached full mast again, and with his arms around her, rolled them both over so that he was on top. His hardness pressed against her mound, and her legs parted, inviting him in. He groaned in helpless desire, settling his groin in the warm cradle between her thighs.

She raised her knees, accepting him fully, and his heart pounded as the tip of his cock plied her waiting entrance, reveling in its soft wetness before plunging home. He wanted her answer, wanted her unconditional acceptance of what he already knew in his heart and soul, that their joining was beyond marriage, beyond any permission or sanction, because they were fated to each other, irrevocably.

"Say it, Marly. Say you love me. Say you'll marry me." He felt the rapid rise and fall of her lungs beneath him as she panted in and out, as heated with desire as he. Her soft brown eyes had darkened into needful pools of dark chocolate.

"Only if you promise to make love to me like this every day," she gasped. "That it will always be like this between us."

"I promise," he whispered, cupping the underside of her breast and massaging it gently. His cock eased forward then retreated again, teasing the slick, hot tissues of her sex.

"Oooh," she groaned, writhing in anticipation. "Make love to me, now, please…"

"Is that a yes?"

"Yes!" she squealed, her fingernails digging into the meat of his shoulders like cat's claws and her hips bucking upward, begging for more of his throbbing cock. He didn't disappoint her, a smile on his face at her answer. He thrust deep inside her, again and again, just as he'd imagined all those months ago. The girl who haunted his dreams was real at last, was his at last; and would be his from this day forward. He needed no priest or judge to pronounce that.

*

A haze hung in the air and stretched across the midafternoon sky, the relentless sun paling behind it as Marlena and Tristan began the journey back to Zaragoza. They'd stayed far longer than intended, consummating their mutually pledged union a few more times before admitting it was time to leave. Tristan was as uncertain as she on what awaited them on their return home, but they'd made their choice and no power in Spain or anywhere on Earth would separate them nor defeat them.

They enjoyed some tapas in the cantina before officially checking out of the seedy but nostalgic establishment. Tristan saw no-one in the place that resembled the gypsy behemoth that had attacked Ariel on his fateful last visit here, and no-one appeared to recognize him; just another faceless gringo in the crowd. Joints like this rarely cared where or who the money came from as long as your drinks and lodging were paid for.

With full bellies and a carton of sodas for the road, they set off for home. The van's gears ground and the suspension squeaked as he backed onto the cobbled lane behind the cantina to turn around. The place looked even more neglected in daylight than it did at night. Of all the places he could have returned to, this shabby bar was not on his list; but now that he had happy memories of it to wipe out the unpleasant ones, it would always remain special.

He glanced over at Marlena seated on the passenger side, to find her gorgeous brown eyes already staring back at him. He'd never forget this day, or how beautiful she looked despite everything they'd been through. The day the rest of their lives would begin. "What?" he said, smiling at her deliberate gaze.

"Tell me about Aunt Juliana," she said. "About what happened here. About your friend."

Tristan shifted the van into drive and the vehicle jolted forward. Of unpleasant memories, El Mirador certainly topped the list and wouldn't make for very pleasant conversation. The images he still held in his mind were horrific at best. He wasn't sure if she was ready to hear the whole truth, but it was a fair drive to Zaragoza, and she did ask the question.

As he navigated to the main highway leading out of the city, he thought about how to begin, how he could put aside the image of Juliana's now-scarred body and tell of the beguiling, spirited girl that had set such unthinkable events in motion. "I remember her red hair. You couldn't help but notice her with that flaming red hair," he said, a smile forming as he pictured her at her most beautiful.

Marlena smiled and nodded. "Yes. Everyone noticed that about her."

"I was hitchhiking, and my friend picked me up on the highway just outside Segovia. I'd been looking at ancient architecture there. He drove a fancy car, and I could tell he had money. He was flashy; a big talker. He wasn't afraid to tell me about himself and his business."

"What was his business?"

"Tourism, I guess you'd say. He owned a few properties on the north coast, and was on his way to the Costa Del Sol where he'd just bought another venture. I think you know the name."

Marlena nodded. "El Mirador. Mirador means a place you can see out from. A viewpoint."

"Yes, it was all of that. A beautiful view of the sea. But it was a long drive, so we ended up stopping at the cantina. We had a lot to drink, and suddenly there she was, her red hair flashing as she danced a flamenco. Ariel couldn't take his eyes off her."

"His name was Ariel?" Marlena asked, her eyes widening.

Tristan nodded. "Ariel Torres."

"My tía wouldn't say his name; only that he was handsome, and he tried to grab her."

"I think he attracted people more with his personality than his looks. It was magnetic, and impossible to ignore. You could fill a room with his charisma."

"What did he look like?"

"Black hair, well-groomed, a moustache and tanned skin. About six feet tall, and dark eyes that held you hypnotized in their gaze."

"It sounds like women would find him irresistible. No wonder my tía fell for him."

Tristan chewed his lip for a moment. There was an attraction, certainly, but in the end, a fatal one. He wasn't entirely sure how deep Juliana's feelings went, considering how cruelly she'd jilted Ariel in the end. "But he got very drunk and put his hands where they didn't belong. She left the dance floor, but Ariel followed her out back. I told him to stay put, but he wouldn't listen. I went out the front entrance and circled around into the alley. That's where I saw this hulking big gypsy rag-dolling him around, about to pound the life out of him."

"You mean a Romani. They don't like to be called gypsies. What did you do?"

"I wasn't any match for the…a Romani his size. I hadn't any weapons, but my backpack had a steel frame and was full of all my gear, so I slid it off my back and swung it at him from behind. It caught him in the head and he staggered sideways before falling to the ground. He'd let Ariel go, so I grabbed him and we legged it."

"When did you see Juliana again?"

"Not for a few months. We drove through the night to El Mirador. I thought we'd part ways at that point, but he offered me a job, more or less. We got on well, and he was grateful for what I'd done. He wanted to train me in the resort business, and open up a casino inside the hotel. He even talked of becoming partners but…" he let out a bitter chuckle. "It wasn't in the cards, so to speak." He looked over at Marlena, who had turned her head to gaze out the passenger window. "Things went really well for awhile," he went on. "I helped with repairs and such, and business was good. A lot of jet-set money flowed through there, celebrities and rich tourists. Then one day, this redheaded girl showed up, begging for work. Ariel recognized her right away, despite how thin and pale she'd become, like the fire had gone out of her."

"She was ill? Was she injured?" Marlena asked in alarm.

"No. I just think she was starving. Ariel took pity on her and gave her a job as a dancer in the hotel nightclub. It wasn't long before they were lovers."

He glanced at Marlena for a reaction. She nibbled nervously on one of her fingernails. "Did he ever plan to marry her?" she asked.

"I don't know, but he was certainly besotted with her. He hired her to dance, but became more and more jealous whenever she performed in front of a crowd. She didn't like that, and…"

"Is he Jorge's father?" Marlena interruped, her full attention turned to him. "This man?"

Tristan tightened his grip on the wheel. Now that he'd actually seen the baby, he had no doubts that was true; but Ariel would have had no such assurances. "In my opinion, yes. Jorge looks very much like him."

"Then what happened? Why did he not protect her from harm, if she was carrying his child? What kind of monster was he?"

He didn't blame her for the anger he heard in her voice. Juliana had suffered terrible injuries, but her family didn't have all the facts. "I mean no disrespect to your Aunt, but she had other lovers. No-one could be certain who the father was. Ariel, he couldn't see past his jealousy or his feelings of betrayal. The night it happened, he caught her in bed with another man. Their bed. In their room. He went crazy with rage."

Marlena swallowed hard. "Go on."

"He couldn't control his anger. I followed him into the basement, where there were a lot of gas fumes, and…he had a blowtorch in his hand. I tried to reason with him, I begged him not to…" Tristan broke off, his words seeming to die in his throat, choking him into silence.

Marlena reached out and gripped his arm. "Are you saying…he set the fire himself? Deliberately?"

Tristan nodded. "When I knew I couldn't stop him, I ran. I had to save her, save her baby…" Recalling the awful ordeal again in such detail left him sweating and anxious. He rolled down the window for some fresh air, but a ferocious blast of wind made him recoil inside the cab. Dark clouds had gathered overhead, roiling and churning like slow boiling water and blocking out the sun, the daylight taking on a strange, greenish hue. Marlena's face looked paper-white against the gloom, and he couldn't blame her for paling at the story he'd just told. He took a deep breath as he closed the window. "His uncontrollable passion destroyed everything, including himself."

"Incendio," Marlena murmured.

"What?"

"Incendio. It means fire. That's what my Tía Juliana said, Incendio; and that I'd end up like her, consumed by flame, because I told her I would brave anything, even fire, to become a famous model." Her voice wavered as she spoke, then put a hand to her forehead.

"It's just words, Marly; nothing like that will ever happen to you. I'll be with you, keeping you safe." She nodded and wiped at her face before looking up at him. His heart clenched at the sadness and fear in her deep brown eyes that glistened with tears, and he knew he'd give his life, his immortal soul to protect this girl; his girl, his future wife. The van swerved slightly, buffeted by the wind. Tristan gripped the wheel and steered them back on course. The weather seemed to be worsening as they drove north. "Let's get home," he said. "There's a storm coming."

Chapter Twenty-Two

"I really must be going. Thank you for your hospitality," Ernesto said, rising from his place at the Ibanez' small wooden dinner table. The meal had been satisfying, as had the company; but nothing would be solved by his staying any longer.

"De nada, you will always be welcome here, Senor Alvarez," Carolina said. "I hope you find your friend Senor Flynn; it would be terrible if something has happened to him. Ángel has grown very fond of him."

Ángel beamed a smile across the table. "He teaches me things, and cares about me. That's what a father does," he said proudly. "I wish he'd come back."

Ernesto raised his eyebrows at the boy's comment. "I'm sure your own father cares about you, Ángel," he said.

The boy dropped his gaze. "Ángel's father passed away when he was very young," Carolina explained, rubbing Ángel's shoulder gently. "We are grateful for Senor Flynn's help."

"Then, I'll have to look extra hard to find him," Ernesto said, forcing a smile. There seemed no use in fighting it. Flynn had bored his way into the very heart of their town like some parasitic worm. He imagined squashing that worm under his boot when he finally did find him.

"Ángel, see Senor Alvarez out, por favor," Carolina said, gathering the dishes into a stack as she remained seated in her chair. He gazed at the wheeled contraption, noting its construction. He could have easily built something like it himself if anyone had asked; but they had not asked. Once Flynn was gone—and Ernesto was certain he would be gone as suddenly as he'd arrived, leaving everything and everyone he'd touched high and dry—he could take his place. He could play El Milagro as well as any man, maybe better, because he belonged here.

"It was nice to meet you, Senor," Ángel said, hopping to his feet. "Come again, any time."

"Gracias," Ernesto said, and turned to follow Ángel. As they reached the door, an ear-shattering crack of thunder rocked the house, rattling the dishes and silverware on the table. The boy dropped to the floor in fright, covering his ears.

"Ángel," his mother called, wheeling her chair toward him.

Ernesto crossed to the nearby window and looked out. A darkened sky threatened overhead, and rapid bursts of lightning flashed from behind the thick clouds. His pulse quickened as he thought of Marlena caught in the oncoming storm somewhere. Was she safe? Was she frightened? He wanted nothing more than to protect her, but was helpless to do so under the circumstances. He felt angry at his own inabilities, his lack of bravado and ambition; all the things that Marly seemed so to admire and did not find in him.

Another resounding crack of thunder shook the floorboards beneath his feet. He shifted his balance just in time to avoid being speared by shards of glass as the window suddenly shattered. He heard Carolina scream, and turned to the sound. She held Ángel's head in her lap as he kneeled next to her chair, her eyes wide with fear. "Can you help us, senor," she said. "Take us somewhere safe?"

"It's just a storm, it will pass," he replied, unsure where he could take them. Surely it was better to remain indoors rather than venture outside, especially with Carolina's mobility issues. He gazed in shock at the broken window. "I'll clean up this glass," he offered, spying a straw broom in a corner of the kitchen. As he moved toward it, a nasty gust of wind blew through the opening, forcing more glass out of the frame and a plume of dust into the room. The thin curtains flapped wildly. He turned to the frightened boy and his mother. The humble dwelling had not even a partition behind which they could shelter. "Is there something we can use to board up that window?"

Carolina shook her head. "What you see is all we have."

"Any tools? A hammer?" he asked.

"No, nada."

Ernesto sighed and looked around, his eyes falling on the solid wooden table. He lifted the stacked dishes and placed them on the floor, then upended the table and dragged it to the window, bracing its broad flat top against the opening. "I'm sorry, but this will have to do for now." It didn't cover the window entirely but was enough to keep out the wind. He picked up the broom and began sweeping the glass into a pile.

"It's all right, thank you, senor," Carolina said.

Ángel had risen to stand next to her. "It will get cold in here," he said anxiously. "And what if it rains? Cold and wet is not good for my mother."

Ernesto looked at him and pushed up his eyeglasses in frustration. "If your roof is solid, it should keep out the rain. Turn on your stove and open the oven for heat," he suggested. "I don't know what else you can do."

"Take us to the church," Ángel pleaded. "There is plenty of room, it's warm and it's made of stone. We'll be safe there."

"Ángel," Carolina said, taking her son's hands in hers. "We can't ask that of Senor Alvarez. I'm sure he wants to get home to his own family."

Ernesto thought of his family, his farmhouse with warm, comfortable rooms and plenty of food, in contrast to the mother and son in front of him who had little except each other. He hadn't thought to tell anyone where he was going since he'd left home yesterday. His kin would be just as worried about him as he was worried about Marlena, and a stab of guilt sliced through him for not considering them. In fact, he hadn't considered anything except his own rampant emotions for days. The Gracia Immaculata would be right on his way home, and there was nothing to be served by staying in town. He'd exhausted his options to find Marly. He couldn't help her, but he could help these two people. "It's a good idea. I can take you to the church," he said. "Ángel, help your mother to the door while I bring my truck."

Ángel nodded as Ernesto turned to leave. The front door groaned with the pressure of the wind against it as he opened and hastily slid through it. The wind's force took him by surprise and nearly knocked him off balance as he stepped out. It whistled through the thick curls of his hair, lodging sand and dust against his scalp. He saw food wrappers and other garbage fly past him down the street as he staggered around the corner to where he'd parked. It seemed like Mother Nature was having a temper tantrum and taking it out on the world around him. He heaved himself into the truck's cab to escape her wrath.

The engine came to life without difficulty and as he drove around the corner, Ángel was already watching for him through a crack in the door. He came to a stop in front of the house and jumped out to open the passenger side of the truck. Ángel held his mother's arm as she attempted to step out onto the street. Ernesto ran to her other side. "Por favor, we must hurry," he said, lifting Carolina into his arms and depositing her into the cab.

"She needs this," Ángel shouted over the howling wind, trying to yank the wheelchair over the threshold.

"I've got it," Ernesto growled, returning to grab the metal contraption with both hands and practically hurling it into the truck bed, irrationally annoyed that he had to rescue his rival's little invention along with the boy and his mother. Ángel scampered inside the cab next to Carolina and pulled the door shut. Shielding his face with one arm, Ernesto moved to the driver's side and got in. "Is everyone all right?" he asked.

"Yes, we are fine," Carolina said, but her pale face and worried expression seemed to say otherwise. "We are sorry to be such trouble."

Ernesto shook his head, inadvertently sending dust flying as it shook loose from his hair. "It's no trouble, senora. You'll be safer at the church, and perhaps Pastor Giorgio will have some news." He pulled away from the curb and started back though town the way he had come. They saw few people about, and those they did see were hurrying for shelter, bracing themselves against the unruly winds. The clouds had turned an ominous blue-black, giving the tortured streets a ghoulish, surreal cast that turned day into night.

A jagged finger of lightning stabbed through the sky, and a ripping crack of thunder followed, audible even inside the truck, the reverberation enough to jostle the vehicle itself. Carolina ducked her head as Ángel clung to her. "Why is there no rain?" the boy asked suddenly.

Ernesto's lips tightened as he considered the question. He'd never seen a storm quite like this one. Heavy cloud cover, with lightning and thunder almost always brought a torrential, even if brief, downpour. Everything about this storm was unusual, even with the extended drought that had gripped the Zaragozan plains of late. As they reached the town square, El Guardián's stark white trunk and barren branches stood out against the dark backdrop of sky, as jagged and forbidding as the bolts of lightning that flashed all around it.

He stepped on the brake to make the turn for the church, when one of the streaks of lightning seemed to lash out like a giant sword and slice the tree's helpless, brittle arms. Sparks flew as a felled limb snapped and crashed to the ground. The three looked on in horror as smoke and a flicker of flame rose from the charred stump left behind.

"Don't stop," Ángel cried.

Ernesto had no intention of stopping and hit the accelerator hard, his tires spinning as the vehicle careened through the turn and Carolina's chair slammed hard into the wall of the truck box. If there were no rain soon, the relentless wind might carry those sparks aloft, and he didn't want to picture where they might land. Everything around the tree, including shops and homes and fences, would be ready, ripe targets for a hungry fire.

Soon, the silhouette of the Gracia Immaculata came into view and he pulled the truck to a stop in front of its main doors. "Ángel, go open the doors and I'll bring your mother in," Ernesto said.

"There's a back door," Ángel said, pointing around to the side of the building. "It will be easier, and I'm sure the Pastor will let us in."

Ernesto hadn't ever been through the back door, and kicked himself mentally for not remembering there was one. Although he was certain he could do it, carrying Senora Ibanez up those stone steps, as light and petite as she was, would be difficult as well as unsafe. He steered the truck around the side Ángel indicated.

At the back of the church was a small gated yard that connected to the cemetery. As Ernesto pulled up, Ángel leapt from the truck, pushed open the unlocked gate and hurried up the path to knock on the wooden door at the rear of the building. They were sheltered somewhat from the wind back here, but the menacing clouds still roiled overhead.

In a moment, Don Giorgio appeared. "Why Ángel, what brings you here young man?"

"There's a storm coming," Ángel replied, his young voice breathless and full of urgency. "It blew the window in at our house, we needed to come someplace safe. Can we stay here?"

Don Giorgio placed a calming hand on the boy's head, then looked past him toward the truck, his weathered face lined with concern as he noted the occupants. He nodded at Ernesto. "Of course. You are all welcome here; please come in."

Ángel scurried back to the truck to help Carolina climb out. Ernesto unloaded the wheelchair and placed it near her. The Pastor ventured down the path toward them, glancing upward to the darkened sky. "This is most alarming. I've never seen anything like this weather," he said. "Is everyone alright?"

"We're fine," Ernesto said, holding the chair steady as Carolina settled into it with Ángel's help. He frowned and glanced up to meet Don Giorgio's eye. "But Marlena is still out there somewhere."

The Pastor shook his head and turned to Ángel. "Go on, take your mother inside. I must speak with Senor Alvarez."

Carolina reached out to touch Pastor Giorgio's arm. "Gracias, Padre."

Don Giorgio gave a warm smile in reply as Ángel began to wheel her inside. Then he spoke quietly to Ernesto. "I have no news of either Senorita Sanchez nor Tristan. Did Ángel know anything?"

Ernesto shook his head miserably. "No. He hasn't seen him since yesterday."

The Pastor sighed. "I presume you are still harboring your original suspicions, then?"

"I can't help how I feel, Padre."

"Well now," Don Giorgio chuckled. "Can't blame you for that. We wouldn't be human without our feelings, would we? Unfortunately, there's nothing we can do but wait. You've done what you could, son. Come inside and rest. Have something to drink. Pray if you want to."

"I can't stay, Padre, but we may need your prayers. Something far worse may be happening, and I have to go see. Help if I can."

"What are you talking about?"

"On our way here, we saw lightning strike El Guardián and catch flame. I'm afraid the town may be on fire."

Chapter Twenty-Three

Flashes of lightning illuminated the forbidding black clouds like bombs bursting inside them. Broken tree branches lay strewn across the road, ripped free by the fierce winds that seemed to blow from all directions at once. Twigs and other debris struck the windshield as they drove forward. Tristan held the van on course, his knuckles showing white as he gripped the wheel hard.

The city of Zaragoza loomed up ahead, its skyline obscured by a sickly gray haze. Marlena kept her eyes on the strange tableau before them, and gasped as streaks of lightning lashed out from the clouds and skittered across the horizon in a wild, jagged pattern.

"Holy shit," Tristan muttered, bracing himself for the expected report of thunder. Marlena covered her ears in the same anticipation. None came. "This is so weird," he said after a moment. "Lightning but no thunder; clouds but no rain. And the wind is warm, not cool. It's like no storm I've ever seen."

The inside of the cab had grown chokingly hot, the windows having been rolled up for almost the entire trip. Sweat clung to Marlena's neck and rolled in between her breasts; her dress felt stuck to her skin and her legs bonded to the cracked vinyl of the seat. By the time they reached her villa she'd look as bedraggled as a stray cat, and give her family all the more cause to suspect the worst. "How much longer until we get there," she asked, wiping her brow with the back of her hand.

"Maybe a half-hour," he said. "To the city limits. We'll have to cross town to reach your villa or else go around somehow."

"Whichever is the fastest," she said, wondering if the storm had already hit the outskirts of town and wreaked havoc on the farm. Suddenly she was more worried about her family than herself; and felt guilty that she'd not been there to help. Perhaps she'd never get away from this place, never be free of family responsibilities to live the life she truly wanted. But Tristan had changed all that irrevocably. She had to move forward, not back. By her own actions, the new course of her destiny had been set, even if it wasn't quite the way she'd imagined it.

Mile after anxious mile passed, until they were near enough to the city to realize the murky haze than hung over it was not cloud, but smoke. Its acrid smell permeated the inside of the van, sneaking through any and every available crack or vent hole. Marlena put a hand over her mouth. "Incendio," she said. Her mind raced, bits of her conversation with Juliana coming back to her in flashes, as menacing as the lightning now ripping the sky, the runaway train of her thoughts arriving at a single destination. "I've brought this...I'm the cause of this," she moaned.

"What?" Tristan said, his eyes breaking from the road ahead and flicking over to her. "What are you talking about?"

"I told you what my tía said. I would end up like her. Consumed by flame. Because I asked for it, dared it to try and stop me from reaching my dream. And I've brought it down on all of us, on everyone!"

"That's crazy," Tristan said. "We don't even know it's a real fire, it could be just someone burning brush, or…"

"It's not!" Marlena cut him off. "You don't know my tía. She sees things, knows things. We have to get to the villa, now! Please!"

"Okay, calm down," Tristan replied. "We'll cut around the city on side roads, there might be traffic or blocked streets if we try to go through."

"Just hurry," she cried, leaning forward and gripping the dash.

Tristan turned onto a dirt road that veered to the east, only slowing enough to make the turn before accelerating even faster than they had been traveling on the highway. The vehicle's rusted springs protested as the two of them were jostled wildly about by the rough, unpaved surface beneath their wheels. "Hang on," he said unnecessarily. "I'm sure everything and everyone at your villa is fine," he added. "And it's ridiculous to blame yourself. Fires don't start spontaneously by divine wrath, or whatever you may think is at work here."

Marlena turned on him. "Haven't you read the Bible?"

Tristan blew out a breath. "Yes, okay, I get your point. But its not very likely that the hand of God reached down and struck a match, now is it?"

Marlena bit her lip and decided to say no more on the subject. They could discuss religious beliefs another time, and his flippant remark made her wonder if that would be something to come between them in future. She'd bucked against tradition, but it didn't mean she would abandon her beliefs entirely. The van hit a deep pothole and tossed her upward to bump her head on the ceiling of the cab. "Ow!" she cried, and grasped about for another handhold as she came down again.

"I did say hang on," Tristan said as he gained control of the wheel again. "Are you okay?"

"Fine," she grumbled, rubbing one hand on her head. "I don't care if you think my beliefs are silly. I just know I'm part of these events, just as you think you know I'm not."

"I'm not questioning your beliefs. And I do know your tía, by the way. What do you mean about her 'knowing things'? Are you saying she's some kind of clairvoyant?"

"Everyone in the family says it. She has visions, premonitions."

Tristan stayed silent for a moment. "She didn't seem to have a premonition about El Mirador," he finally said. "She'd have gotten out on her own if she knew something bad was about to happen."

"Maybe she did know," Marlena said, thinking back on other conversations with Juliana. Was it possible her aunt had felt she deserved to die by fire? And made no attempt to save herself? It felt too horrible a thought to contemplate; and if fire had come to their villa, would Juliana feel as though the flames had returned to collect their due after she escaped the first time?

"What?" Tristan asked.

"It's in the past now," Marlena said, then raised a finger to the window. "Look, the smoke is getting thicker."

Tristan nodded. "And it's not coming from out in the country. Seems more like…oh, bloody hell!" he exclaimed as they neared an intersection with another unpaved road that pointed north toward town. He slammed on the brakes to make the turn, the force of it throwing Marlena against the passenger door. "It's coming from the town square!"

Marlena righted herself and brushed away a stray lock of hair from her face. The square. The markets, the shops, the church! All of these stood within blocks of it. The months of drought had made everything ready tinder, and this surreal lightning storm provided just the match to ignite it. It would only be a matter of time before it spread to her home, if it hadn't already.

"I'll take you home," he said. "Then I have to see what's going on, Don Giorgio might be in trouble."

Marlena felt panic rising, but not because of the danger that might lie ahead. She needed to get home, yes; but if Tristan were to just drop her off, it would be like a repeat of the day he brought Aunt Juliana home, only worse. Tongues would wag even more viciously, and he wouldn't be there to defend her honor, explain what happened and his intentions. He'd look like a villainous cad who would be reviled and never accepted or trusted again. That might be worse than not showing up at all. "Then I'll go with you," she said.

Tristan looked her way again. "I thought you wanted to get home. And you should. We don't know what we'll find in town."

Marlena gazed back at him, hearing his words, but not listening. She took in his roughened appearance, his days-old clothes, his piercing blue eyes and wild blond hair; his lean, slightly dirty hands on the steering wheel. Wondrous hands, full of strength yet capable of exquisite tenderness. He would always protect her, and thought he was doing so by taking her where she'd be safe. But by staying with him now, she could protect him, too. From suspicion and rebuke, from rejection by her family. She could protect their future. "I know. But we will face my family together, not apart. And whatever we find in town, we'll face that together too."

A tired smile lit his handsome face. "We will," he said, nodding, then turned his attention back to the rutted track ahead of them. The few scattered farm sheds and outbuildings they passed alongside the road indicated they were nearing town. The smoky haze continued to descend, reducing visibility and obscuring their path forward. A railway track bordered the town, and after they'd crossed, followed a back road that skirted past the square and led them in the direction of the Gracia Immaculata, its stony silhouette barely visible until they were almost upon it.

Tristan pulled around to the back of the building and got out. Marlena didn't wait for him to come to her aid, and jumped out of the passenger side. The air, thick and sharp with smoke, stung the back of her throat as she breathed in. She covered her nose and mouth and hurried through the gate to the church doors, with Tristan right behind her.

He pushed the door open and ushered her inside, quickly closing it behind them. The darkened rectory lay empty except for a few plates and cups on the long table. From the sanctuary she heard voices, one at least she was certain of. Don Giorgio's. Tristan's hand slipped into hers and pulled her toward the sound and the church's inner sanctum.

Don Giorgio stood on the dais leading a prayer. Several people seated on the pews nearest the front bowed their heads and repeated after him, as well as a woman sitting in what looked like a wheelchair directly in front of the dais. Together, she and Tristan moved forward down the center aisle. The Pastor signed and concluded his prayer as they drew near. Reflexively, Marlena dropped Tristan's hand and repeated the sign. He glanced at her and then up at Don Giorgio.

"Tristan," the Pastor said, a relieved smile crossing his face. "Thank goodness you've returned…and Senorita Sanchez as well. It is very good to see you both."

All heads turned to them, and among them Marlena saw the faces of her mother and aunt in the front pew, with Jorge cradled in Juliana's arms. She rushed forward to embrace them all. "Mama, Tía!" she exclaimed, throwing her arms around them. "I'm so sorry. Are you both alright?"

Juliana cast a knowing eye over her, and then over Tristan. She gave Marlena a small nod, but kept silent, turning her attention to the gurgling infant in her arms. Bianca, her face pale and eyes reddened from crying and likely irritated by the smoke, reached out to stroke Marlena's cheek. "Cariña, thank God you're safe." Her expression held no anger, only relief and gratitude.

"I'm fine. Tristan was with me," she said. "He helped me get home." Bianca's gaze drifted over Tristan, then back to her daughter.

"So, it's true you were together," she said. "Ernesto insisted that you were."

"I'm sorry, Mama, for lying to you, and not telling you where I went. But I started off alone; I hadn't planned on being with anyone. Tristan only happened by and offered to help. Ernesto couldn't have known anything about it."

"Ernesto cares for you, he always has, you know," Bianca said. You worried him as much as us. He went looking for you everywhere. You should apologize to him as well."

"Where is he," Marlena asked, glancing around at all the people gathered in the church. Ernesto was definitely not among them.

"He went back to the square, to see what was happening and try to help. He said that lightning struck El Guardián and it caught fire. He saw it."

Marlena put a hand to her mouth. Her nightmare had come true, and she was the cause of it. The drought-ravaged town would go up like a torch, and the fire could spread to the open grasslands if not caught in time. "What are you both doing here? Is the villa safe?"

"Yes, it's fine. José and the boys dug trenches just in case, and will use water from the livestock troughs if we need to. We came here to pray for your return," she said.

A heartbreaking sob echoed in the high-ceilinged sanctuary and all eyes turned toward the sound. The blond woman in the wheelchair held her face in her hands, her shoulders trembling, with Tristan crouched by her side.

"Poor thing," Bianca said. "As though life hasn't been cruel enough to her already."

"Who is she," Marlena whispered, watching Tristan as he spoke softly to the woman and put a hand on her shaking shoulders. Then he stood and walked toward Marlena, his face laden with concern. He took her hand in his as he stepped close, then turned to acknowledge the other women.

"Senora Sanchez," he said to Bianca with a nod, and another to Juliana. "I'm sorry I can't stay and talk. I want you both to know that your daughter did nothing wrong, and is a strong, courageous girl. I'm grateful to have brought her home safely. Please take care of one another until I return. We can answer all your questions then."

"Where are you going," Marlena asked in alarm. This wasn't the plan; they'd promised to face everything together from now on.

"I'm going back into town," he said, squeezing her hand gently. "I have to find someone. He could be in danger."

"Ernesto's gone there," she said.

"I know; that's why I have to go. Ángel ran off after him, and hasn't come back."

"Ángel?"

"That woman's son," he said, gesturing to the woman in the wheelchair. "He's only ten years old, and he's all she has."

Marlena looked over at the blond woman, obviously distraught over her son. "How will you find him? Do you even know what he looks like?"

Tristan exhaled deeply, then nodded. "He's one of the first people I met here. He asked me to build that wheelchair for his mother," he explained. "She can't lose him, and neither can I. He's my friend."

To Marlena's surprise, he leaned in and kissed her full on the lips, right there in church for all to see, including her mother. Oh, there'd be hell to pay later; but what did appearances matter now? He was going to save a little boy, and Ernesto, maybe the whole town, and why not? He'd saved her already. That's what heroes did.

Chapter Twenty-Four

Tristan drove the van as near to the town square as he dared before pulling over and continuing on foot into the chaos of the main street. The sun had long set by this time, but the smoke and dust hanging in the air blocked any view of the moon or stars overhead. He took the shovel that was still in the van along; if necessary, he could use it to dig a firebreak or smother runaway sparks with dirt, or worst-case pry someone or something free from under a collapsed structure.

He made his way into the square, and saw for himself what Ángel's mother said was true. Flames billowed up from the naked branches of El Guardián, searing them into a spindly spiderweb of glowing, red hot twigs. Rivers of fire flowed out along the tree's gnarled roots and snaked across the cobbled pavement in multiple directions, fueled by the fierce wind setting flame to dried leaves and litter. Shops on every side of the square had already caught fire, flames licking at their cloth awnings and searing their doors and windows black. Where was the bloody fire department, he wondered?

He coughed, and shielding his nose and mouth, strode forward. A moment later, he was relieved to see some flashing lights through the thick veil of smoke. Thank Christ, at least some kind of aid had arrived. He made his way toward the lights, and found a small crew of men moving around an emergency vehicle, pulling hoses and connecting to a nearby hydrant. "Hey," he called out to them. "Can you use some help?'

A man who appeared to be in charge turned to him, the angled features of his moustached face illuminated in the glow of flames. "Senor, stay back please. You can help us best by keeping yourself and others away from danger."

"I understand," Tristan said. "but you need able bodies. I'm volunteering."

Unwilling to spend time arguing with him, the man strapped his hat tighter to his head and gestured to the adjacent street leading out from the square. "Clear those buildings," he said, make sure no-one is trapped inside. The wind is carrying the smoke that way."

Tristan nodded and hurried in the direction he'd pointed. He looked back over his shoulder at the blazing firebrand that was El Guardián. His efforts to try and save the historic icon had been in vain. With bitterness, he realized he should have let them cut it down; perhaps this whole event could have been avoided. He'd wanted to build something beautiful in this land, and here he was doing nothing but destroying it.

He pushed aside these thoughts, and forged ahead down the street the fireman had indicated. He soon understood why. This street was lined with homes and apartments. Through the smoky haze he glimpsed a sign that read Calle Verdugo. As he shouldered his heavy shovel and trudged forward, he was suddenly almost knocked to the ground by something or someone barreling into him from the side. He stumbled under the impact and lost his grip on the shovel.

"You!" The man shouted. "What are you doing here? What have you done with Marly? If you've laid a hand on her I swear to God..."

Tristan recognized the voice immediately, despite the rasping hoarseness caused by smoke inhalation. Ernesto. "She's at the church," Tristan shouted back before Ernesto could finish his threat. "She's with her mother, and Don Giorgio, and others. She's safe."

"What did you do to her? Where did you take her?" Ernesto carried on as if he hadn't heard a word, pouncing on him as he tried to regain his footing and knocking him fully to the ground.

"Stop," Tristan yelled, rolling to one side to get up, but Ernesto landed on him with his full weight and pinned him down. The breath was squeezed from his lungs, and he gasped like a suffocating fish, with nothing but smoke-laden air to inhale.

"I'll kill you if you hurt her in any way," Ernesto snarled. "Or maybe I'll kill you just to be rid of you." Tristan gagged for air while struggling to throw his assailant off. Ernesto's slight build wasn't heavy, but with his lungs starving for oxygen, Tristan couldn't budge him. He'd underestimated the depth of the man's resentment for him.

He groped for the handle of the shovel he'd dropped. He didn't want to injure the man, but had to do something to bring him to his senses. Ernesto lunged for his outstretched arm and tried to restrain it, but Tristan's fingers had already closed around the smooth wooden handle. He dragged the instrument toward him and swung it upward. The bottom side of the blade caught Ernesto in the shoulder. He grunted and was knocked sideways. Tristan rolled loose from under him and got to his feet, staying in a low crouch and holding the shovel crosswise in front of him.

Ernesto staggered to his feet, seeming dizzy from the blow but not seriously injured. His glasses were nearly off and hanging from only one ear. He straightened them as he rose to his full height, his chest heaving as he too, gasped for breath.

"Are you crazy," Tristan shouted. "If you really want to kill me, you'll have to do it later, assuming we don't both die by fire first, you idiot."

"Where did you take her," Ernesto asked again between coughs as he advanced on Tristan again.

"Nowhere she wasn't already going," Tristan answered, bracing himself to take Ernesto's weight as he lunged clumsily toward him. Tristan drew the shovel handle up to chest height and forced Ernesto back with a quick outward thrust of his arms. Ernesto swayed on his feet but kept his distance, too short of breath to continue. "She's not your concern anymore, amigo."

"What do you mean?" Ernesto spat.

"She's made her choice. If you care for her, you'll respect that. Now listen to me; Ángel is missing. Have you seen him?"

Ernesto stood back, a stunned look on his face and his shoulders sagging like a man too beaten down to resist any further. He took a few wheezing breaths. "He's at the church, too. I took him there myself. You were probably too busy ogling my girl to notice," he sneered, still stubbornly combative despite the situation.

Tristan shook his head. Arguing with the man was pointless, and a waste of precious time. "Ángel isn't at the church," he shouted over him. "His mother told me he ran out after you. Now, have you seen him, or haven't you?"

Ernesto seemed to regain his wits. He pushed his glasses up the bridge of his nose, their lenses coated with ash and dust. "No, I haven't seen him," he replied. "I've been at the well, with others, to try and bring water from there, but it looks like you fucked that up too. There's barely anything coming out."

The mention of the well triggered Tristan's mechanical brain. He recalled the painstaking work he'd done to restore the well's flow and then diverting some of it underground to almost this very spot. It had only been a trickle at the start, but perhaps it had gained pressure since then, and would explain why the flow at the well itself had lessened. Buckets would likely not fill fast enough for the carriers to do much good, if hauling it by hand was what they had in mind. If he could release the water pressure in the underground pipe, it might be enough to at least keep the ground moist and slow down the fire's spread; but the idea would have to wait. "I have to find him. The fire officials asked me to evacuate the homes on this street," he said, pointing with the blade of the shovel.

Ernesto looked in that direction, his mouth forming a grim line. "Ángel's house is on that street."

"Bringing water from the well by hand will take too long. I have a better idea. Help me clear the street and look for Ángel. Then I'll show you."

Ernesto ran a hand through his curly hair, shaking loose a cloud of dust, then wiped his brow with his sleeve. "I'll take the side with Ángel's home. You take the other," he said.

They separated, and Tristan quickly checked all the houses on his side. Most were empty, but the few residents who remained heeded his order and left. He doubled back to meet up with Ernesto, unable to see more than a few feet ahead. His eyes, nose and throat felt as thought they too, were on fire. They couldn't breathe this air much longer. "Ernesto!" he called, his voice stifled by the smoky, acrid air. He kept his feet moving and called Ernesto's name again.

"Here!" he finally heard in response.

Following the sound, Tristan came to a small abode with its window smashed and its door wide open. He stood on the small porch and peered in. "Ángel! Ernesto!" he called. Footsteps crashed toward him, and Ernesto appeared out of the dimness.

"He's not here," he said, pushing past him to get out onto the street.

"Where would he go? Any ideas?"

"How should I know? You're his damn fairy godfather," Ernesto said. "I only met the kid today."

Tristan bit back a retort. He hadn't done anything intentional to make Ángel look up to him, but certainly got the impression that Ernesto now felt he had to compete for the boy's affection as well as Marly's. He began to understand the man's frustration. How would he feel if the situation were reversed? Bloody pissed off, he imagined, but now wasn't the time to be adversarial. "We'll keep looking," he said. "But we have to move on. If we don't get that fire under control, everyone is in danger, not just Ángel. I have a plan, and I need your help. Let's get back to the square."

Ernesto didn't look at him, but nodded in agreement. "What's your plan," he asked gruffly as they began to jog side by side back to the heart of the disaster.

"There's another way we can use the well water," Tristan said. "A few days ago, I set up a pipeline leading from the well to El Guardián. It's underground about a foot, but we should be able to dig it up. The flow wasn't much at the time, but passing through a small-bore pipe would have built up the pressure by now. Let's hope it's enough."

An unholy glow filtered through the veil of smoke as it hung over the square. The two hurried their steps, short-cutting their way through narrow alleys to reach the open area surrounding El Guardián. As he watched the flames curling up its trunk in a fiery spiral and billowing outward along its thick lower branches, Tristan realized that the place where the pipe ended was much closer to the tree than he thought.

The fire crew's efforts seemed to be focused on the buildings that surrounded the square, leaving the tree to burn unhindered. Indescribable heat radiated from it, singeing his skin right through his clothing as Tristan raced across the square with Ernesto on his heels. The brightness of the flames lit the entire square, and he had no trouble locating where he'd last buried the pipe; but as he got near the spot, his steps slowed. The backfilled earth he'd laid down just days ago had been disturbed, scraped away in a haphazard pattern, as if dug by bare hands.

Ernesto nearly piled into him as he stopped short, and then a shriek of terror raked his ears, audible above the roaring din of fire. Tristan looked up, and to his horror there was Ángel, terrified and clinging to a sagging telephone pole, it's base charred and weakened by the fire. It could collapse any minute, and the urgency of excavating the pipe suddenly seemed secondary. He didn't know how or why the boy got there, but someone would have to climb up and get him down. "Ángel!" he called out. "Hold on, I'm coming!" He took a step toward the pole and was quickly jerked back by a firm grip on his arm.

"You've got the shovel," Ernesto said, his dirty eyeglass lenses eerily reflecting the menacing flames. "Do what you came to do. I'll get the kid."

Tristan stared at him for the space of a heartbeat, then nodded. "Go." He watched him dash toward the pole, and then turned away. He had no choice but to trust Ernesto's agility and strength to rescue Ángel, no matter how much he wanted to do so himself. He gripped the shovel and dug furiously in the face of the flames that were quickly advancing on their position.

The firemen were doing a good job suppressing the burning buildings, but until they quashed the source of the fire they'd still be at risk. He worked faster, until he felt his arms shudder as the blade of the shovel struck something solid. He started scooping the dirt away like a madman, widening the trench to get at the pipe and create a path to direct the water.

Sweat seemed to stream from every pore of his skin as he began chopping at the makeshift pipe to split it open. The heat was tortuously oppressive. He could barely see or hear anything, but sensed movement nearby. As he looked up, Ernesto appeared out of the smoky haze, carrying Ángel in his arms. Thank Christ. He set the boy down and he immediately scrambled toward Tristan. He laid his shovel aside for an instant as Ángel threw his arms around him. "I knew you would save me," he cried.

"It was Ernesto who saved you," Tristan said, wanting to hold on to his lanky little body but prying himself loose because of the intense heat. "What in God's name were you doing here," he admonished, trying to sound stern but not quite managing it. "You should have stayed at the church!"

"I wanted to help! I tried to follow Sr. Alvarez but I couldn't find him. I remembered the pipe I helped you make," he said. "I thought I could dig it up and make the water go out on the street. But my hands got tired, and I had to get up high to get away from the smoke."

"So, you climbed a telephone pole," Tristan scolded.

"Come on, let's get this thing open," Ernesto interrupted. He dropped to his knees and began clearing away more dirt with his hands. Ángel tried to help, though his hands were nearly raw. Tristan chopped at the pipe one last time, and the casing burst open. As though his prayers had been answered, streams of water spewed forth from the broken pipe with all the forceful pressure he'd hoped for.

The trench they'd cleared funneled the water outward, spilling out onto the ground and then reaching the super-heated brick pavers of the square. Steam rose and mixed with the smoke, the 'holy' water snuffing out everything in its path as it raced toward El Guardián. Tristan gave a shout of triumph and looked about for his tiny apprentice, only to find him clinging to his new hero. He smiled and stood back, ignoring his protesting knees and aching back to watch the flames smother and start to die.

Then he felt something land on his head. On reflex he swatted at it, thinking it may be a spark that would set his hair on fire. Then he felt another on his arm, then another. Something trickled down his scalp. By God, it was starting to rain. "It's raining!" he shouted needlessly, spreading his arms wide and welcoming each drop as it struck his skin. He basked in the cleansing sensation of it as the rain increased, regretting his sarcasm about the wrath of God. Ángel may call him El Milagro, but they had all just received a true miracle, literally from on high.

Chapter Twenty-Five

Baby Jorge gurgled happily as he lay snug in his mother's arms. Marlena smiled at him, but could feel Juliana's unwavering stare fixed on her, rather than her son. She met her aunt's intense gaze, a knowing glint in Juliana's green eyes that said she knew everything Marlena had done since yesterday, and felt a shiver course up her spine. She could also feel her mother's quiet wrath settling upon her, for her actions, her deception, and most of all, the very public kiss she'd just enjoyed.

Bianca interrupted her and Juliana's wordless exchange. "Sr. Flynn said he helped bring you home, Marlena. Home from where?" Her tone seemed to balance somewhere between concern and condemnation. Marlena faced her mother. How would she explain this without Tristan here to back her up?

"Madrid. I went there to see about a job."

"A job?" Bianca asked, as though not hearing her daughter correctly. "What sort of job?"

"A modeling job, and the ad said I could only apply in person. I had to go, mama, I just had to."

"Why couldn't you tell me this? Instead of making up lies?"

"I didn't think you'd let me go if I told you. And, if I got the job," Marlena paused and lowered her eyes. "I wasn't coming back."

Bianca stayed silent for a long, uncomfortable moment. "I take it that didn't happen," she finally said

Marlena shook her head. "No. They…were no longer hiring," she said, wincing inwardly at yet another lie, but it was better than the truth.

"And how is it that Sr. Flynn found you?" her mother persisted.

"I was going to take the bus to Madrid. He saw me at the bus stop, and offered to drive me instead." Marlena looked up again, sensing Bianca's disapproval. "It would have taken hours and hours on the bus," she said in defense.

Bianca regarded her intently before speaking again. "Then why did you not come home until today?"

"It got late," she said. "We stayed in a hotel in Madrid."

Bianca's jaw dropped in disbelief. "You…" she began, but couldn't seem to find any further words.

Juliana placed a hand on Bianca's arm. "It is all right, sister," she said. "I foresaw this. It was meant to happen. You needn't be upset, nor worry."

"But, that… just isn't done," Bianca gasped, then closed her mouth as several people cast curious glances her way. She leaned in, and lowered her voice. "We'd planned for you to go to modeling school, not run off at the first chance you had. How could you do that to us? To yourself?'

"I can't wait for the school to make up its mind. I can't stay here forever, mama," Marlena pleaded. "I want to make something of myself, and I want to do it now. For me, for you, for Jorge." She glanced at Juliana. "I'm sorry, Tía Juliana. But you know what will happen here. He will always carry your shame; be denied opportunities because of what he is. I don't want that for him."

Juliana diverted her gaze to her baby, and they all fell silent. Working up her courage, Marlena knew she had to say the rest. "Mother. There's something else. Tristan wants to marry me."

Bianca looked into her daughter's eyes. Behind their dark irises, so much like her own, Marlena saw a storm of emotions; shock, confusion, sorrow. But there was also happiness. Taking in a long breath, Bianca pulled something from her purse. "This came for you today," she said, handing it to Marlena.

Marlena took the slightly creased, white business envelope from her mother and looked it over. It wasn't very thick; perhaps only a single sheet of paper inside it. Then she noticed the return address; from the Escuela de Modelaje, and she nearly stopped breathing. The modeling school had replied! A bittersweet stab of agony sliced through her. If she'd only stayed at home one more day; if only she hadn't been so impatient, she wouldn't have caused everyone so much grief. But if she'd stayed, she'd never have found her destiny with Tristan. He said he'd never hold her back, but would this letter change things?

She tore it open and pulled out a sheet of crisp letterhead. She forced her hands to stop shaking as she unfolded the letter, and got as far as the first line before squeezing her eyes shut.

Dear Sra Sanchez. We regret to inform you...

No. No, no! It couldn't be. After all this waiting, she was being rejected? Disappointment bubbled up in her throat until she felt it would choke her. As she sat there wishing away the words on the page, a pattering sound began overhead, amplified in the tall space of the sanctuary. It grew stronger, and heavier. She opened her eyes. The people began to stir, looking upward and murmuring prayers of thanks. Pastor

Giorgio went to one of the windows and opened it. Praise the Lord, it was raining.

Suddenly, the doors to the sanctuary burst open, and all eyes turned to the intrusion. In the archway stood Tristan, and behind him Ernesto, who carried a young boy in his arms. All three looked as though they'd been through a war; sodden and covered in dirt.

"Ángel!" the woman in the wheelchair cried, holding her arms out. Clearly this was her missing son, the boy Tristan went to find; but it was Ernesto who brought him forward, carrying him several steps before setting the boy's feet on the floor. He ran to his mother and collapsed into her embrace. Their joyful sobs echoed in the stillness of the church while murmurs of relief rippled through the small crowd.

The two men hung back, then slowly approached the front of the church. Ángel's mother lifted her blond head to greet them as they came near. "Thank you, thank you both," she said, her voice choked with emotion.

"He's alright, Carolina. Just a few scrapes. He might have a cough for a few days," Ernesto said, gently ruffling the boy's hair. Marlena watched the scene, struck by how different Ernesto seemed with his clothes and face tarred with soot and the purposeful confidence in his stride as he had come forward, playing the role of hero. Suddenly she no longer saw him as the boy she'd grown up with; he was a man in his own right, and he deserved better than the way she'd treated him, no—used him—in the last few months. She regretted it deeply, and hoped he'd find his own path, the path he was meant to follow, and be happy. If that still meant staying in Zaragoza, working for his family and in the community, then that was all she could wish for him. His choices were his own, and not up to her. She had no right to pressure him.

Tristan walked toward where she sat on the pew behind her mother and Aunt Juliana. Marlena caught his gaze, his sparkling blue eyes hollowed and red-rimmed, but still reflecting the warmth and deep meaning of what they'd shared. Tía Juliana had known from the beginning, that he would bring great change, for both good and bad; but all of it was right, for her, for him, for her home town, even though it might be already razed to the ground. Incendio.

"What's happening?" she asked as he stood over her. She set the letter down as he reached for her hands and pulled her to her feet.

"The fire is under control," he said evenly. "But we lost El Guardián, and a lot of the surrounding buildings. It will take a long time to repair."

"Perhaps it takes destroying some things, to make way for better ones," she said, thinking not only of the town, but of her crushed dreams. He threw her a curious look, then pulled her close and cradled her head against his chest.

"Yes. Sometimes that is what it takes. No-one was hurt, but it's a huge loss for the community. Things will never be the same again. That's why I have to help."

"You've done all you could. It's not your responsibility," Marlena said.

"Yes, it is. I was drawn here for a reason; for many reasons. I know it now more than ever." He rested his chin on top of her head and held her even tighter. "That's why I'm going to stay."

"Stay? At the church?" she asked.

Tristan chuckled, the warm vibration of his chest tickling her cheek. "I mean here in Spain. Unless you have an objection."

"I don't," she answered, her mind a jumble of excitement, apprehension, uncertainty. What would this mean to their relationship? "But what about England? Your family?"

He grinned and stroked her hair. "I told you when I came to this country, I didn't know my purpose; what I would do with my life. But I began to see what was possible, and now I see what is inevitable. I'm needed here. To build. And rebuild. And to be with you."

Marlena felt tears welling as he spoke, realizing in that sliver of a moment that becoming a model was not everything; that what she also wanted was to be with Tristan, in the place she knew her heart would always call home. Still, it was not that simple. "You can't sleep in Don Giorgio's shed forever. Where will you live?"

"Where will we live," he corrected her. "To know that, there's someone I need to ask." He released her from his embrace, and focused on Bianca, who had been watching them intently. Marlena wasn't sure if her mother looked pleased or horrified, her face seemed so pale and her eyes like crystals of black ice. "Senora Sanchez. I said I would answer any questions you have; but would you be so kind as to let me ask one first?"

Bianca and Juliana exchanged glances, then Bianca gave a nod.

"I wish to marry your daughter," he said. "And you should know that she has already said yes and I'm going to marry her regardless of your answer, but I'm told it's traditional to ask your permission. May I have it?"

Marlena drew in a sharp breath. She wasn't expecting him to just blurt it out like that. She held the air in her lungs as she waited for Bianca's reaction. Aunt Juliana averted her eyes, seeming very pleased with herself as her lips formed a satisfied smile. Onlookers had started turning their attention to the scene.

With practically the whole church watching her, Bianca cleared her throat, then proudly lifted her chin. Her eyes ticked back and forth between Marlena and Tristan, and a smile tugged at the corners of her mouth. "You may have it, Senor Flynn. Welcome to our family."

Marlena exhaled, and re-filled her lungs with a breath of joy. Applause and congratulations flowed from all around them, and she and Tristan kissed again in full view of everyone present, including the Pastor and Ernesto. When their lips separated, she caught a glimpse of Ernesto over Tristan's shoulder. He stood near the little boy and his mother. The film of dirt on his lenses hid his eyes from her, but his facial expression seemed blank, resigned.

She'd plunged the final dagger to his heart, and it looked as if he was too numb to even feel it. "What happened between you and Ernesto?" Marlena asked, whispering in Tristan's ear amid the many voices all around them.

"I hit him with a shovel."

"You what?"

"We had a disagreement," he continued. "But we saw eye to eye in the end."

"You got in a fight?"

"Just a small one. It didn't last long. 'Only a fool fights in a burning house,' as they say, or in this case, a burning town." His expression sobered. "Pretty much the whole square was on fire, we had to move fast. We worked together despite our differences. He's a good man, Marly."

"I know. And I've hurt him so much," she said, shaking her head. "I need to apologize. He didn't deserve the way I treated him."

"You told him the truth. That's what good friends do."

Yes. He had always been her friend; her rock. She had to be that for him now. Ernesto stood, rigid and unmoving as she strode toward him. "Ernesto," she said softly.

Ernesto didn't move. "I'm glad you're safe," was all he could say.

Marlena's heart recoiled at his coldness; he seemed like a stranger, not the lifelong pal and confidante she'd always known. "I'm sorry for all the pain I've caused you. You know you will always be in my heart, just not the way you'd hoped. If you no longer feel friendship for me, I understand."

Ernesto shook his head, and gingerly removed his glasses. The look in his eyes, so full of tenderness, pain, and longing, nearly broke Marlena's heart. "That isn't possible," he said. "You are part of me, Marly. That will never change. I love you. I've always loved you; but if all you have to give me is friendship, I will gladly accept that."

Marlena felt her heart twist at his words. They could not be plainer. He loved her; and loved her enough to let her go. She would never have a better friend. She wrapped her arms around him and hugged him tight, not caring about the dirt and ash that covered nearly all of him. "Thank you," she said.

Epilogue

September, 1973

Tristan stopped working long enough to appraise and enjoy the vision before him; marveling at the delicate curves of her cheekbones and the arch of her brows; her flawless skin and sleek dark hair. He drank in all her loveliness, knowing he would have a lifetime ahead to appreciate it. It made him smile.

"I brought your lunch," Marlena said, setting a basket down on a makeshift workbench that consisted of a sheet of plywood straddled over sawhorses. Tools and plans littered its surface, and construction materials lay everywhere around them, lumber, sheeting, concrete blocks, wire and conduit. The repairs to most of the storefronts in the square were progressing well, and the construction company Tristan had started was lining up more and more work every day. Even after the repair work was completed, they'd be busy until the end of the year. It was a small venture, but Tristan knew it would lead to something much bigger. The name Flynn Enterprises had been floating in his brain and had a nice ring to it. Someday he'd incorporate it.

"You are an angel of mercy," he said, clearing a spot on the temporary workbench.

"No, I'm the devil of details," she replied, unwrapping the basket. "I still want your opinion on the flowers and invitations for our wedding; but since you hardly have time for me anymore, I'm stuck with the decisions. I hope this isn't a pattern for us going forward." She flashed him a disapproving glare, but a wry smile curved her luscious lips that he couldn't wait to be kissing again. In private. Or not.

It's true he'd been busy, but it was all for their future. One day he'd have armies of workers under him and would take his soon-to-be bride on trips around the world, spending as much time with her as she'd allow before getting sick of his doting attention. "I trust your judgement completely," he said, then turned and whistled across the piles of lumber and over the noise of power tools. "Ernesto! Lunch!" He turned back to Marlena and reached for a sandwich from the plate she'd laid out on a tablecloth. "Aren't you due at school soon, young lady?"

She handed him a napkin. "Not until Monday," she said. "They've only just received the enlargements I sent. I'm lucky that the letter said my application had only been put on hold until I submitted my full-length portfolio pictures."

"We're lucky there were some useable pictures in that camera," Tristan said, taking a bite. Although it represented an unpleasant incident, they decided to develop the film taken from the fake studio in Madrid. The first few shots of a clothed Marlena were actually pretty good. They had them made into 8x10s and destroyed the rest; they even got a decent price for the camera at a local pawn shop.

Ernesto joined them at their temporary table, doffing his hardhat and gloves. Tristan had been very impressed with Ernesto's natural aptitude for carpentry. After seeing his work on some of the farm buildings at the Sanchez villa, he asked him to join his construction crew for the town repairs. He'd shown himself to be a reliable, fast worker who took on responsibility readily. With formal training, he'd be an even greater asset to the little company; which wouldn't remain little for very long. Tristan envisioned it growing far beyond Spain's borders.

"This is wonderful, Marly. Thank you," Ernesto said as he looked over the lunch spread.

Tristan watched him say a silent grace before helping himself to the food. A good man, to be sure; gracious enough to let the best man win, and smart enough to grasp opportunity when it presented itself. It seemed like the right time to pitch the idea he'd been mulling around. "Ernesto, would you be interested in becoming more than a carpenter?" he asked.

Ernesto pushed up his eyeglasses and regarded Tristan for a moment. "I suppose so. Why do you ask?"

"Because, I was thinking you'd make a great project manager, maybe even a design engineer."

Ernesto seemed taken aback. "Kind of you to say, Tristan, but I'm happy being exactly what I am. Just ask Marly," he said, throwing her a shy smile. Marlena tilted her head and returned the smile. It didn't bother Tristan that hers and Ernesto's friendship remained solid. He might be possessive about certain things, but not this. He admired and respected them both too much to interfere with their choice of friends.

"I'm glad," Tristan said. "But, if the opportunity to study engineering came along, wouldn't you be interested? With a degree in your pocket, you could work for any company, anywhere in the world."

"My world is here," Ernesto replied. "And I could never earn a degree. Who would accept an application from an uneducated, self-taught carpenter like me?"

"Oh, I don't know about that. If you had a sponsor, say an alumni of a respected engineering school in Wales, you could be accepted quite easily. And when this job is finished, you'd have enough money for tuition. What do you say?"

"You're offering to sponsor me?" Ernesto asked, repositioning his glasses again. Marlena squealed and clapped her hands in delight.

Tristan looked around, to his left and right and over his shoulder. "You see anyone else blathering?" he asked.

Ernesto blew out a breath and shook his curly head. "It's a lot to think about."

"While you're both thinking so hard, why don't we all take a walk after you've eaten and talk it over," Marlena said.

"Good idea," Tristan said, wolfing down the last of his sandwich. Marlena packed away the remains of their lunch, and the three of them strolled around the square, discussing the extent of the damage and the progress of the many repairs. Ernesto asked questions about the university and Tristan answered them, but said he wanted more time to consider the opportunity.

"The offer is open whenever you decide," Tristan said. They eventually came to the center of the square, as though saving it for last. Tristan still found it hard to look at the blackened, sawn-off stump that was all that remained of the once massive, flourishing tree. He smiled as he thought of Ángel and his declarations that the tree would never die, and that it was older than any of the people who lived here. The boy had taught him much about life here, despite his lack of years.

"It was a very old tree," Marlena said. "But I believe that old things must die, if there is ever to be room for the new. Don't you agree?" She looked over at both men.

"Yes, I can see that," Ernesto said, his gaze lingering on her, his interpretation of her statement painfully clear.

Tristan filled his lungs with the sharp autumn air that still held the bitter tang of destruction. Incendio. He remembered

Marlena's words. Consumed by flame; just like his heart in his desire for her. "I agree," he said, considering the omnipresent conflict between old and new. Between ancient trees and newly planted forests; between old traditions, and new ways of thinking. "It's happening all around us. Not just to El Guardián or this city, but across the country, with your own government; and the change will be welcome."

Marlena crouched down to examine the remains of El Guardián more closely. "Look!" she said, pointing to a spot on its flat-topped stump. He and Ernesto leaned in for a closer look, and to his astonishment, Tristan saw that a tiny green shoot had erupted from somewhere deep inside the ancient sentinel that refused to give up its life. Its spear-like tip defiantly awaited its moment to unfurl into a fully formed leaf.

He shook his head in amazement. The new, rising from the ashes of the old. It fit. This hot-blooded land he had embraced in all its passionate glory would experience a new beginning, forged from the rich depths of the old, just as he himself would; with a new family to cherish and an empire to build.

- THE END -

Other books by Jean Maxwell:

El Mirador
(Spanish Seduction 1)

El Precio
(Spanish Seduction 2)

Indecent Proposal
(Workplace Gone Wild Book 1)

The Witch Doctor
(Nine Lives Chronicles Book 1)

Winter Symphony
(Overtures Book 1)

From the Author

Thank you for reading this book. I sincerely hope you enjoyed it, and if so, the favor of a customer review would be appreciated.

*

Stop by my official online hangouts and say hello!

idreamofjean.com
facebook.com/authorjeanmaxwell
@dearjeanmaxwell

*

Yours in words,

Jean Maxwell

www.ingramcontent.com/pod-product-compliance
Lightning Source LLC
Chambersburg PA
CBHW032001180726
48283CB00008B/2523